Through the Mirror Door

SARAH BAKER

Catnip
PUBLISHING LTD

For Rachael,
who said I really should write these stories down.

CATNIP BOOKS
Published by Catnip Publishing Ltd
320 City Road
London
EC1V 2NZ

This edition first published 2016

1 3 5 7 9 10 8 6 4 2

Text copyright © Sarah Baker, 2016
Cover illustration copyright © Jessica Courtney-Tickle, 2016
The moral rights of the author and illustrator have been asserted.

Cover design by Will Steele

A CIP catalogue record for this book is available from the British Library.

ISBN 978-1-91061-1036

Printed and bound by CPI Group (UK) Ltd., Croydon, CR0 4YY

www.catnippublishing.co.uk

Chapter One

'That was your last chance.'

I stared at the worn carpet till my eyes blurred.

'You brought this all on yourself, you know.'

I looked up. 'So?' I mumbled.

Mrs Morrison sat behind her desk. She patted her fluffy hair as if checking it still sat on top of her head. 'So . . . I can't keep you here any longer.' She sighed. 'It's not just the running away and the fights. You went too far this time. You really frightened the little ones.'

I stared at the carpet. Pale brown threads had come loose and wriggled across it like worms.

'It was just a story,' I said to the floor.

Her voice softened. 'My hands are tied, lovely. I have to move you on.'

I looked at her out of the corner of my eye, then at the old black-and-white picture of the kids' home above her head. It had slipped sideways in its frame and looked like it was sinking into the pale blue wallpaper.

Abandon ship! I thought, but they were the ones abandoning me.

Mrs Morrison shook her head. Her hair wobbled.

'Right then. I'll call your key worker and we'll get the paperwork started. A new home might be just the thing. You can start again. Make some friends this time.'

Outside the rain had begun to slide down the window. 'Angela?'

'I don't care,' I said, shrugging.

'You don't care about the key worker, about leaving, or about upsetting the other children?'

I was thinking about telling her it was all three when the phone rang. Mrs Morrison picked it up. She looked at me and frowned.

'Hang on.' She put her hand against the mouthpiece. 'Angela? Give me five minutes.' She nodded towards the door. 'And no running off.' She spoke into the phone. 'Yes, I understand. I mean, that's . . . well . . .' She let out a breath. 'That's very timely.'

Mrs Morrison's words washed over me as I grabbed the door handle. I'd heard it all before. *We can't keep you here. A new home will be good for you. It'll be a fresh start.'*

'I'll get started on the paperwork right away.'

I pulled the door open.

'Wait!' Mrs Morrison put the phone down and beckoned to me. 'Good news, Angela. Change of plan.'

I looked into the corridor where two boys were kicking a football – and each other. Three loud thuds came from above, shaking bits of dust from the ceiling onto the carpet. Someone was getting thumped. I was just glad it wasn't me. I rubbed at a bruise on my arm.

'Shut the door, Angela. Take a seat.'

When I turned round Mrs Morrison was beaming, which was weird. I'd never seen her smile like that. She usually just looked tired.

'I think we might have an opportunity for you.'

I frowned. I didn't care about the new kids' home I'd be sent to. It would be exactly the same as this one. And the one before.

Mrs Morrison leant forward. 'Your aunt and uncle are going to take you on holiday for a few weeks.'

My mouth dropped open.

'Oh, I'm not supposed to say it,' Mrs Morrison said, clapping her hands together, 'but, Angela, they might be able to take you on after all.'

Mrs Morrison started looking for something on her desk, lifting papers and opening and closing files.

I felt as if something had got stuck halfway down my throat. I only had one aunt and uncle, and they hadn't bothered with me since everything happened. They hadn't phoned, they hadn't visited and, even though I was supposed to go and live with them, they'd said no and I'd ended up in a home. So why would they want me to go on holiday with them? And why now? I wasn't sure I even wanted to see them again.

'Angela?'

I looked up.

Mrs Morrison opened out her arms. 'One last chance, after all.'

Chapter Two

A week later I was at an upstairs window, watching a silver car sparkle in the morning sun as it as it struggled down the drive over hardened muddy ruts. As it bounced closer I saw my Aunt Cece and Uncle Vaughn in the front. There were two smudges of blond behind them – my cousins, Kitty and Fliss. I wondered why they were really here and why now. What changed their minds about me?

They parked in front of the peeling wooden gate that leant over bleached grass right next to the car on bricks, which had started to rust. They peered through their windows at the terrace of three houses, which had been left squatting on their own, as if the rest of the street had upped and left one night. Nobody got out of the car.

'This is a good opportunity, lovey,' said Mrs Morrison, handing me my rucksack. 'You should make the best of it.'

The bell rang for lunch and I let the curtain drop.

Mrs Morrison was chatting as we walked downstairs, as if she hadn't just told me for the hundredth time that this holiday was a test – a *compatibility test*, she said. But I knew what she meant: behave. Mess it up and I'd be sent to another kids' home. And it would probably be miles away. Not that I'd miss anyone in this one. I rubbed my arm again, tuned Mrs Morrison out and concentrated instead on her fluffy hair, freshly streaked on Monday, her day off. She was wearing the tweedy jacket that was too small for her and a wilting curl of pale pink blouse crept out from under her collar. The rest of us were in shorts and T-shirts.

'Angela? Did you hear what I said?'

I nodded, but I hadn't made up my mind yet which was worse – another kids' home or making my aunt and uncle like me enough to keep me.

'So you understand?'

I didn't understand anything. Mum had hardly ever talked about her sister except to complain about the once-a-year visit, and my aunt and uncle hadn't bothered with me at all since I'd been in care. My cousins were always mean when we'd been to their house. Now they were all taking me on holiday to France and, if I managed to be completely perfect, they might just let me live with them after all. I shrugged. They wouldn't want me. Not even if I was on my best behaviour. Not if they knew what really happened.

'A summer holiday is a good thing, isn't it?' She leant forward. 'And family is family.'

'They're not family,' I said.

'Angela,' she warned.

A boy in a stained striped T-shirt waddled out of the TV room. As Mrs Morrison picked him up, a stream of snot dangled from his nose.

'Chelsea?' she called over his head, then muttered to herself, 'Where is she?'

As she looked for the new support worker she shifted him to her other hip and the slithery line of snot swung, twisted, then broke off. I gagged.

'A word to the wise, Angela,' she said. 'You need to think about getting on with people if you're ever going to fit in anywhere.' She tried to pat my arm, but I ducked away. Her voice hardened.

'You might be a bit grateful to them, too.'

She looked at the boy. 'Plenty of kids don't have any family.'

'But they're not family,' I said. 'Not family-family. They don't care about me, they never did. I don't know why they're suddenly so interested.'

The boy in her arms started wriggling. Jamie, I think his name was. The door to the kitchen opened, releasing a cabbage-and-beans smell that wafted towards us and made me cover my nose. Heavy thuds above us turned into chants of 'Fight, fight, fight!'

Mrs Morrison raised her eyes to the ceiling and started towards the stairs, then she turned back as if she'd forgotten something.

'Angela?'

I crossed my arms over my chest.

'This holiday is a chance for you to have a family, a home. So take the opportunity to have a think about what you really want.'

I rolled my eyes.

'Make friends.'

She looked up at the ceiling as if to say the kids here could have been my perfect BFFs if I made the effort. As if she didn't know the only reason I wasn't in a scrap right now was because I was with her.

'Otherwise, you'll have to go somewhere else. You can't come back here.'

My chest felt tight. Anger burnt through me so fiercely I thought I could see it.

'I don't care,' I muttered.

Mrs Morrison opened her mouth to say something else when bloodcurdling screams came from upstairs. The car outside beeped three times. The lunch bell rang for the second time. She closed her eyes for a few seconds.

'I bet you wish I'd died too, don't you?' I said, biting my lip so I wouldn't cry. 'Then none of you would have to bother with me.'

I picked up my rucksack and ran out the front door, slamming it as hard as I could.

Chapter Three

Outside it was quiet, which sucked some of the anger out of me. Well, almost. Aunt Cece had opened her window and I could hear the tinny rhythm of my cousins' iPods as they sat in the back of the car looking totally bored.

'Everybody sit tight,' she was saying, 'and remember what I said.' She gestured to the house. 'We'll just wait here. I don't want to have to go inside that place if I don't have to.'

Suddenly she clocked me standing there, nodded, then busied herself with a lipstick and mirror, painting on a dark pink smile. Like every time I saw her, I wondered how she and my mum could have been sisters. She was thin and pointy where mum was soft and smiley, and apparently Aunt Cece wore a suit even on Saturdays, when mum lived in jeans. I wasn't sure my aunt even owned a pair of jeans.

Uncle Vaughn got out the car and gave me a wide grin, showing off what looked like a small fluffy creature clinging to his top lip. In the six months since I'd seen them all last he'd swapped the hair on his head for some under his nose and his shirt was now stretching to breaking point round his stomach. He opened the boot and I dragged my legs forward. He was being friendly. Maybe it would be okay.

Kitty sat up as I approached. She was older than me by thirteen months and taller by a few centimetres, which she used to insist on reminding everyone. She was pretty (and she knew it), but the permanent frown line between her eyes made her look as if she thought everyone else was something disgusting on her shoe – the look which I'd just got full blast. Not a great start. Fliss was a month younger than me, with hair a slightly dirtier shade of blond than her sister, but just as long, and she still seemed to have a thing for pink clothes. When she saw me coming she drew her legs up onto the back seat so there was no more space.

Kitty looked me up and down then sank back into the seat. 'Hello, catwalk queen. Love your vintage look,' she said.

Uncle Vaughn laughed, as if he hadn't caught what Kitty'd really just said, and reached for my rucksack. I held on to it for moment, and we had a sort of tug of war. He won, and wedged it into the tightly packed boot. Then he ruffled my hair and opened the back door.

'It's really brave of you to dress so differently,' Kitty added. 'I so couldn't pull off wearing such old clothes,' she added and laughed.

But as I got in the car she shifted away from me with a loud huff and Fliss stared at the floor without moving, so I was forced to climb over her to get to the middle, which everyone knows is the worst seat ever.

Aunt Cece looked at the house and gave a nod to Mrs Morrison who was now waiting in the doorway. Uncle Vaughn got in and started the engine. As the car drove away my aunt winced every time a clod of dried mud hit the window.

'Your clothes have such an interesting smell, Angela,' Kitty said.

I began to pick at a loose thread on my jean shorts. I'd made them myself from the pair of jeans I'd managed to save. They'd only been a bit damaged. I'd had to borrow my vest top, cardigan and shirt from the home, but the pocket patch on my shirt came from the T-shirt I'd been wearing the night it happened. It was the closest I could get to anything that was mine from before. My stomach twisted. Kitty was being Kitty, but this wasn't that different to being in the home. They'd picked on me about my clothes there too.

'I can't wait to get our new things for next term,' she sniffed, taking out her earphones and looking at her sister as if I wasn't even there. 'Do you want to look at those boots again, Fliss?' She scrolled through her phone and lowered her voice. 'Mum will definitely let *me* wear them.' She looked at me. 'I mean, I've been wearing heels since I was a kid.'

'Those boots are well expensive,' Fliss was saying.

I closed my eyes and tried to tune them out, but a sharp elbow soon ground into my left side.

'Ow!' I cried.

'What's going on?' Aunt Cece called without turning round.

My cousins sat up straight.

'Mum, I was just making more space for her,' Kitty said. 'You're so sensitive, Angela.'

My fists curled, but I remembered what Mrs Morrison had said about last chances, about making friends and about fitting in. I supposed I had to at least try. Anyway, before I could say anything, both of them popped their earphones back in. I folded my arms, ramming my fists into my armpits instead. The car slipped onto the motorway and its rumble rocked me. My head nodded forward and I felt myself slump towards Fliss. But that's all I remember because one minute I was awake, and the next I was asleep.

And then I was screaming.

I jolted upright.

'Oh. My. God,' Kitty said, looking at me, and laughing.

Aunt Cece turned round. 'Kitty, stop it.'

She squinted at me, then smiled, which made her look like she was constipated. I could see Kitty's shoulders still heaving out of the corner of my eye. Fliss had scrambled as far away from me as she could. Uncle Vaughn cleared his throat several times.

I leant forward, trying to shake off the sounds and the smells of what I'd seen in my nightmare. The sound of me screaming for my dad filled my head and I felt my throat tighten. I dug my fingernails into my palms and took deep breaths. Aunt Cece shook her head and muttered something about behavioural problems. Kitty turned away from me and by the time I sat back, both she and Fliss were lost in their music. Fliss bunched her jumper against the door and leant against it as if she was going to sleep. With a sweet, sickly smell thick in my throat and burning the inside of my nose, I didn't dare.

Chapter Four

I didn't move until we were on the ferry. We got out of the car and trooped up staircase after staircase, with tons of other people pushing ahead and coming the other way, as if no one knew where they were supposed to be. I needed some air and it was easy to slip away in the crush. I took a detour through an open metal door into the middle of the ferry, then kept going round and up the other side until I could get out on deck.

It was raining so I pulled up the hood of my cardigan and leant over the railings to watch the rush of water rolling past the bow. The noise filled my head but it didn't drown out my choices: another kids' home where I wouldn't fit in and probably wouldn't stay long anyway before I went who knows where, or living with my cousins, who thought new boots were the most important thing in the world, and my aunt and uncle who hardly seemed to notice I was even in the car. I sighed. Why had they bothered bringing me?

'Have you lost your parents?'

I jerked back from the railings, but it was only an old couple standing behind me. They were exactly the same height as each other, and wore matching beige macs. They were also wearing the same look of concern. I'd seen it before on Mrs Morrison and felt anger coil in my belly. The old man rubbed his balding, spotted head. The wind kept whipping the few wispy hairs he had left and he smoothed them back.

'It's dangerous to be out here in this weather,' the old lady said, her hair tucked neatly beneath a scarf like the one the Queen wore in a picture they had at my old school. She beckoned to me. 'If you're lost, we can help you find them.'

'I'm not lost,' I said, stepping up onto the guardrails, 'they left me here.'

I let go so I was only balancing on my toes. A thick petrol smell chugging from the back of the boat made me dizzy.

'It's a punishment,' I told them. 'I have to stand out here until I've learnt my lesson.'

The old couple shared a look.

'They'll probably beat me anyway,' I said.

The old lady put a hand to her mouth. Her husband stepped towards me.

'Mum says you have to come inside.'

Kitty was standing in the doorway, her arms crossed, the corners of her mouth turned up. I stepped off the railings, wondering how much she'd heard.

Fliss popped out from behind her. 'You shouldn't go off by yourself – we were worried.'

My face felt hot.

The old man took his wife's arm and led her towards the door, but not before she'd given me what I expect was her best 'disappointed' look. I'd seen that look from Mrs Morrison as well and I was definitely getting used to it. Kitty and Fliss stood aside to let them pass.

'She makes up stories to get attention,' Kitty told them, puffing her chest out. 'I feel sorry for her, actually.'

I turned away and looked at where France would be if everything weren't so grey.

'We didn't have to invite you, you know,' Kitty said, glancing at Fliss, who nodded. 'Mum and Dad just feel sorry for you.'

I wanted to stay outside, let the hurling waves rush into my ears and drown them out. But it was true; they didn't have to invite me and they probably did all feel sorry for me. Most people did, at least at first. But none of them knew the truth. None of them knew what had really happened.

'Fliss? Go and tell Mum we've got her,' Kitty said, 'and

you,' she pointed a finger at me, 'you better get in right now, or I might accidentally tell Mum and Dad what you said to those olds.'

Once we were in France I kept myself awake by tracing our route on the map my uncle gave me, trying to pronounce the unfamiliar names of the tiny villages we passed, until Kitty sighed for the fifth time. The countryside was flat, with long lines of trees either side of the road like ice lollies, each one with the same silvery bark topped with green. I saw a whole field of sunflowers so close to the car it gave everyone a yellow glow. I sank into the back seat, my legs sticking to the leather, my head slipping towards Fliss, then shook myself upright. I couldn't fall asleep again. Not here. It wasn't safe.

Outside it had started to rain. After it got dark I stared into space as the car bumped on cobbles, then over a rickety gravel drive pocked with holes. It reminded me of the road to the children's home. The car dipped and lurched. My stomach flipped, then I sneezed.

Aunt Cece whipped round. 'I hope you're not coming down with something.'

I always sneezed when I was really tired. Mum used to make a joke of it, but I wasn't sharing that with my aunt.

I sneezed again.

She rummaged in her bag and squeezed a gel into my

hands that smelt so sharp it made my eyes smart. Kitty and Fliss shared a look.

'She's fine!' said Uncle Vaughn. 'Aren't you, Angela?' He patted Aunt Cece's leg, taking his eye off the road.

'We wouldn't want her to be ill,' my aunt said, turning back round and brushing his hand off. The car skidded. The brakes screeched and gravel pinged off the doors as we were thrown forward, then back again. Kitty screamed, Fliss shouted, 'Mum!', Uncle Vaughn swore and Aunt Cece glared at him.

'We're here,' he said, clearing his throat and pointing at a wooden sign hanging sideways off a large open gate.

Maison de Noyer, I read. I was going to ask what *noyer* meant when the rain took that moment to turn into a monsoon and the sign disappeared. The car moved on and passed through another gate, across crunching gravel and towards an impossibly tall, dark house. It loomed over us. I counted three floors with eight sets of shutters across each one, making twenty-four windows. But there were no lights on in any of them. Uncle Vaughn stopped the car in front of a huge door squatting in the middle of the house. It was easily twice the size of the ones at the kids' home and looked like it was made of wood criss-crossed with slabs of metal. It really wasn't a house anyone normal would go to for a holiday.

The rain drummed on the roof of the car and streamed

down the windows. I looked at Aunt Cece and Uncle Vaughn. They didn't move and nobody came out of the house.

'We should have rung to say we'd be late,' Uncle Vaughn said.

Aunt Cece shook her head. 'They inherited it over thirty years ago, but still haven't managed to install a phone.'

'Wait,' Kitty said, her face pale, 'does that mean there's no wifi?'

Aunt Cece opened her door. Uncle Vaughn followed and Fliss ran shrieking to the boot. With a glance at me, Kitty ran after her. I looked back at the house, and that's when I saw something.

I was squinting through the rain, half in and half out of the car, when I saw a flicker at the top of the house, slightly off to the left. I thought it was a light at first, but it looked different. It looked like . . . fire!

Suddenly there was a hole where my heart should have been. My feet sank into the gravel, my throat began to close. I wanted to say something, but I couldn't get the words out. Then a face appeared, the glow of fire behind it. It turned and looked straight at me.

A blinding light engulfed us. I blinked hard and when I opened my eyes a huge shadow stood in front of me. Two arms reached out long and spindly towards the car, scrawny fingers stretched like claws.

'Arghhhh!'

'Eeeek!'

Fliss and Kitty had seen it too. Someone grabbed my arm.

'Stop it, girls. Really,' Aunt Cece said, trying to make herself heard over the rain. 'It's only Armuth.'

As the spots slowly disappeared from my eyes, I saw the front door was open, and standing inside was a short, round, middle-aged woman with a man almost twice her height standing behind her. The light from the house had made them looked huge, like monsters without faces. The woman reached out her hand towards the car and its shadow slid across the gravel towards us.

Fliss squealed and clutched me tight, then shook my arm off as the woman's gesture turned into a friendly wave. She waved back.

'*Bienvenue,*' the woman said, beckoning us in.

Aunt Cece started towards the house holding her handbag over her head as an umbrella. The others followed.

'Wait!' I shouted. 'Upstairs! There's a fi—' But when I looked back at the top of the house there was no light, there was no fire and there was definitely no face. The rest of the house was in complete darkness.

Chapter Five

It was dark inside the house too.

I was the last to troop in, soaking wet, my hair plastered to my face and hanging in rat-tails down my back. I'd stood in the rain until Aunt Cece called me in, staring up at the window, willing the face to reappear, but it hadn't.

'I am Armuth,' the round woman was saying, as we dripped inside the hallway. The man behind her didn't say a word. I guessed he didn't speak English.

'I apologise for the mess,' Armuth said. 'Herman and I took on the house many years ago. It's over three hundred years old and it is harder than ever to keep on top of things now.'

Her hair was shaped into a large bun and although it was brown, there was something about her creased face that made her appear ancient. She wore an itchy-looking brown dress with a belt pulled tight around her middle, making her look like a ball squeezed in half. The man was much older, with a peak of thinning grey hair brushed back off his long, pointed face. He was really skinny and tall, and had the longest nose I'd ever seen. He was looking at a faded black-and-white framed picture of a short woman in a white dress and a tall man in a suit that hung at an angle on the wall. It had to be his and Armuth's wedding. When he caught me watching he stared back at me until I looked away.

'It would be worth a lot of money if someone did it up,' Uncle Vaughn whispered to Aunt Cece. She glared at him, then smiled at Armuth, who didn't seem to have heard and was explaining that we'd be staying in the guesthouse out the back.

'Of course,' Aunt Cece said. 'For now.'

Armuth's brow furrowed then cleared as she turned and walked us through the main house. It had dark-panelled corners and old portraits so dirty you could only see an outline of a face or a hand. There were threadbare tapestries on the walls that moved in a draught so cold I could see my breath, and elaborate spider webs above our heads as if they'd built themselves a city. There was an inescapable smell of mildew in the air too. Why would anyone come on holiday here?

'The guesthouse was built from the remains of the

small tower,' Armuth said. 'You will cross the courtyard and find the key in the door, yes?'

Suddenly I sneezed three times.

'Urghhhhhh.'

'Gross!'

Kitty and Fliss shrank into their mother.

'She'll infect us, Mum,' Fliss said.

Armuth looked between me and my aunt.

'I'm fine, I'm fine,' I said. 'I'm just tired.' But then I sneezed three more times and the girls really ramped up their snivelling.

'Of course there's only room for two of the girls in the guesthouse.' Armuth nodded to herself then glanced at me. 'There is a spare room here. It has not been used for some time, but it will suffice.' She peered at Aunt Cece. 'Herman and I never had many guests, so . . .'

'Thank you, Armuth, that will be perfect.'

Then Aunt Cece smiled, her top lip curling. It looked so freaky I took a step back.

'That'll be nice, won't it, Angela?' she said, looking around. 'You can spend some time in this lovely old house.'

'Er . . .' Had Aunt Cece just walked through the same house as me?

But before I could say anything else she began to hurry my cousins away. Kitty skipped backwards, whispering,

'Have fun.' Fliss looked at me from underneath her fringe, eyes wide, before my uncle caught her hand and turned her round.

'Hold on!'

I put my hand out then dropped it again because they'd already gone. Leaving me alone in the oldest, most falling apart house I'd ever seen. Great.

Armuth began to trudge off, disappearing down a dim corridor in the opposite direction. I looked back at her husband, at the huge staircase behind him where I thought the bedrooms would be, but he shook his head and pointed at Armuth. So, still dripping and shivering, my trainers squeaking on the wooden floor, I followed.

She didn't turn on any lights, making it difficult not to bump into her, but eventually she stopped, opened a door and reached for a switch. A thin cone of pale light fluttered to life, revealing a really small bedroom. She told me something in French I didn't understand except for the word *histoire*, which I knew meant history. Then her face softened. She reached out as if she was going to touch my arm, but when she saw me stiffen she changed her mind. She looked behind her, nodded once to me, and left.

I plonked my bag on the nearest of the two white, painted iron cots that looked like servants' beds from a costume drama. There was a pillow like a thin sausage resting on each striped mattress, and a folded sheet and old blanket, but the beds weren't made up. There was a small table between the cots with three books on it. As I lifted the top one, my thumb crumpled into the brown cover, and before I could put it back, pages began to spill out. Pictures of flowers covered with tiny blobs of black mould slipped to the floor and a smell like the inside of an old tent curled up my nose. I stuffed the pages back in as best I could, and shoved the old book at the bottom of the pile. I could feel a draught coming from somewhere and shivered.

The only other furniture in the room was a large wooden wardrobe with a tiny key sitting in the keyhole. I pulled it out and saw something was painted onto the ceramic fob, but it was so faded I couldn't make out what it was. Then, opening the wardrobe, a shudder of grey moths flew out. I panicked and ducked, but they ignored me to circle towards the light, then out of the room.

I looked back in the wardrobe. It was full of old-fashioned clothes: faded smocks and something longer, like a dress. Some of them were embroidered and looked tissue-paper thin. A lot of them were stained. They looked like something out of a fashion history book and I wondered who they belonged to, because they were more my size than Armuth or Herman's. I thought of the face at the window again. Had I really seen someone or was

I seeing things again? It had *looked* real. And it had been staring right at me.

Suddenly a bell shrilled and I practically jumped out of my skin. I looked up to see a strange wire contraption with a ringer attached to it above the door. Talk about old. I glared at it. The bell rang again, but I was ready for it this time, and with a last, puzzled look at the clothes, I shut the wardrobe door, clicked off the light and ran to dinner.

Chapter Six

I found everyone in the kitchen. It was the only place in the house with lights on and the only place that was warm. Old lamps on the walls made the copper pots dangling over the range glow and little pockets of steam rose from the plates of food on the table. My cousins looked fluffy, as if they'd been in a tumble drier. Their hair was washed and brushed and they had clean clothes. Mine still stuck to my skin. I'd spent so long looking in the wardrobe I hadn't had time to change, and I didn't have much to change into. Well, nothing that wasn't borrowed anyway. I knew I must have looked a state because Armuth's husband was staring at me again.

'Ha-hem.'

I turned to Aunt Cece. The cough had sounded angry, but weirdly she was smiling at me again. She'd repainted her lips in a bright shiny pink and opened her mouth wide enough that her teeth peeped out. I sat down quickly. Knives and forks began to clink. Armuth was explaining that we would eat all our meals in the kitchen while we stayed with her.

'There is no sense in opening up the dining room,' she said, looking at her husband, 'and the kitchen is easier to heat.'

I eyed the massive old stove right behind Kitty and Fliss. No surprise they'd got the best, warmest seats in the house.

Everyone else was eating except for Armuth's husband, who must have already eaten because it looked like Uncle Vaughn had his seat. He stood by the sink with his arms folded and nodded for me to help myself. The food smelt rich and my mouth began to water despite watching Fliss edge her fork around her plate and Kitty stuffing squares of meat under a large blob of mash. I tucked in. Luckily it was a beef stew, and tasted a hundred times better than anything we had at the home.

'The library is closed also, yes?' Armuth was saying. 'We saved most of the books in the small salon. It is not damp there.'

She paused and I caught Aunt Cece staring at me. I thought of the books in my room, remembered the one I'd touched, which had practically fallen apart, and nodded. Armuth looked at Aunt Cece too, but by then she had one of her fake smiles back on.

'What about upstairs?' Kitty asked, placing her knife and fork together on a plate she'd barely touched. I sat up and shifted closer.

'Nobody is to go upstairs,' Armuth said quickly, then she gave a long sigh. When she next spoke her voice was almost a whisper. 'There is nothing upstairs but empty rooms.'

Her shoulders drooped. 'In fact, soon all the rooms will be empty. Each generation has struggled to keep the house, sinking time and money into it.' She looked at her husband, then down at her plate. 'But the upkeep is just too much now.'

'Well,' Aunt Cece said, 'maybe it's all for the best?'

Armuth didn't look as if she agreed. 'I do not want to have to sell,' she said, her eyes sliding away.

Aunt Cece glanced at Uncle Vaughn, but he was busy scraping stew onto his fork.

'But perhaps I will find a way.' She looked directly at me. 'A way to save the house.' She gave me a small smile that made her eyes crinkle at the edges. 'I hope for this.'

A shiver ran up my spine that had nothing to do with me being furthest away from the stove. I thought of the face at the window again. Armuth had said there was nothing upstairs, but I'd seen someone, I was sure of it. I shook myself.

Mrs Morrison would say it was my imagination. She always said it was my imagination, if she was being kind, and that I was telling stories and would never make any friends ever, if she wasn't.

'It's what gets you into trouble,' she'd told me, but I knew I'd seen something.

'Angela?'

I looked up. Armuth was offering me more stew. Aunt Cece was smiling so hard it looked like it was hurting her face. The veins in her neck stood out like wires. It was weird she was smiling so much, first at me, then at Armuth. I didn't get it. She managed to keep it going all through dinner and only wavered when Kitty and Fliss murmured half-hearted thanks, not impressed by the books Armuth had just handed them.

Armuth turned to me. 'I have no book for you.' She darted glances between Aunt Cece and me. 'But your gift is something b–'

But Aunt Cece fluttered her hand, cutting her off. 'No need to worry yourself, Armuth. No need at all. I'm sure Angela has plenty of books.'

Her eyes darted to me and she gave a little half cough, half laugh. Then she turned back to Armuth. 'And no need to talk about it in front of the children. It's all agreed now.'

There was an awkward silence.

'What about the land?' Uncle Vaughn asked to cover it, but there was a scrape of chair and he yelled, rubbing his knee, his face white. Aunt Cece shot him one of her death ray looks. Now those I recognised. Armuth gave her husband a small smile before answering.

'With Herman . . . well, there's no one to make the land work.' Her smile faded. 'It is part of the estate. It would sell with the house.'

I stared at Herman. He didn't look ill so why couldn't he help out? But before I could ask, my cousins were getting up to go. I forked green beans, mashed potato and stew into my mouth, and chewed fast.

'Um, wait?' I asked them.

They paused at the door. Aunt Cece, halfway out of her chair, glared because I still had food in my mouth. Oh right, manners.

I swallowed. Now that they'd stopped though, I didn't know what to say.

'Oh my God, Fe-li-ci-ty!' Kitty put her hands on her hips, once she realised what I was asking.

Fliss winced hearing her full name, but when her sister raised her eyebrows, she caught on quickly.

'No way,' Fliss said.

Kitty laughed. 'Yes way. She wants to hang out with us!'

'No, I don't,' I said quickly, stabbing leftover food on my plate with my fork.

'Enough, girls, it's bedtime for all of you,' Aunt Cece said, frowning at Kitty, who turned her laugh into a cough.

'Which is totally cool, isn't it, Fliss?' she said, glancing at her mum, who nodded back. 'I mean it would be the best thing ev-*ver*.'

Fliss nodded quickly.

'I'm fine,' I mumbled.

Uncle Vaughn got up, patted the top of my head and followed her out. Armuth was busy stacking the dirty dishes into the sink. Herman inclined his head from me towards the corridor. I thought about the cold bedroom with its twin cots then I thought about the face in the window. Nobody had mentioned anything at dinner. I had to know if it was real or not. I wasn't sure I could sleep if I didn't check. Herman had turned towards Armuth. I peered out of the kitchen door. If I was going to sneak upstairs and take a look, it was now or never.

Chapter Seven

It was pitch black in the hall once the heavy kitchen door closed behind me. I couldn't see a thing. I thought about the face in the window and tried to shake off the faces I usually saw in the night. I tried not to hear the crackle and spit of flames or smell the thick smoke that threatened to choke me.

I'd almost got to the bottom of the stairs when I heard the kitchen door open and I threw myself behind a large chest, stubbing my toe. I held my breath so I wouldn't shout out. My foot throbbed in time to my heartbeat as Armuth plodded straight past me. I waited a few minutes then eased myself out, flexing my foot. My eyes had begun to adjust to the dark a little, so, taking a deep breath, I followed her fading footsteps. That's when I felt it.

Something brushed my left shoulder.

Something like a hand.

I cringed and pulled away.

'Help!' I screamed, before I could stop myself.

I looked back at the kitchen, but no one came. The corridor was empty.

I heard a screech behind me, then a grinding noise like something settling. I tried to swallow but my mouth was dry. I turned around super slowly, taking as long as I could, then sagged as I recognised the outline of a suit of armour I'd passed earlier.

'Stupid thing,' I muttered, then turned back to look at the kitchen door.

I waited to see if anyone was going to come and tell me off for messing with antiques or whatever, but the house was silent. I was glad I hadn't been caught and everything, but I'd screamed and nobody had come. I wanted to kick the suit.

I tiptoed along the hall, careful to stay in the middle so as not to bump into anything else, but I still heard creaking.

I thought about the suit of armour, my brain going mad thinking there could be something inside it, biding its time, waiting for me to relax so it could get me. I started breathing faster and faster.

Creeeeeeeeak.

The noise was definitely coming from behind me. I

whipped my head round, eyes wide searching for it. My breath coming fast; in, out, in, out.

Creeeeeeeeak.

This time it was coming from ahead of me. I stopped. I couldn't see a thing, but in my head I saw the suit of armour rise up in front, one arm poised to grab me.

I didn't think. I turned round fast and ran back down the hall, trying the handles of all the doors on the way, finding mouldy old rooms, one after the other till I finally found my bedroom. Once inside I pulled the light, but nothing happened. I pulled it again and again. It clicked, but there was no light.

I shut the door behind me then jumped back as the shutters blew open and slammed against the wall. The wind whistled and moaned outside, but they were too high for me to close, even standing on one of the cots. The cold air whispered through and I decided there and then that I would not be getting undressed, and I would not be going to look for the face in the window. It was too dark and the house was too spooky. I slipped off my shoes, grabbed the blankets from the other cot and piled the whole lot on top of me. But even with all the blankets it was freezing.

Suddenly, there was a groan from over by the bedroom door and my eyes shot wide. I stared at the door handle, waiting for it to turn like in all the ghost stories I used to read. But another groan made me realise it wasn't coming from the door; it was coming from the wardrobe. I gulped. The wardrobe door creaked open a little wider, as if in invitation, and I scrambled back on the cot till I felt the wall. I clutched the blankets tight around me.

'Help!' I screamed.

But again no one came.

There was another creak, but from above my head this time.

Creak, creak, creak, creeeeeeak.

I froze. It sounded like footsteps, but Armuth had told us at dinner that she and Herman always slept downstairs, that there was nothing upstairs but empty rooms, which were totally out of bounds. I shivered inside the pile of blankets and let out a sob.

The creaks began to get closer and closer as measured footsteps crept across the ceiling, then stopped above me. I pulled the blankets over my head and screwed my eyes shut.

'It's not real, it's not real, it's not real,' I whispered over and over and over. But fear crawled all over my body, wrapping itself around me and squeezing in through the holes in the blanket. Then the floor above me creaked again. The footsteps were on the move.

Chapter Eight

'Ow!'

Aunt Cece ignored me as she dragged her spiky hairbrush through my tangles.

'I've been itching to get my hands on this bird's nest,' she said, ripping a handful of hair from the brush and letting it drop to the floor. 'And just look at the state of you. It's like you slept in a ditch.'

She was almost right. I felt terrible. I'm not sure I got much sleep at all, listening to the footsteps creaking about and waiting for them to find me, then telling myself they weren't – they couldn't be – real. That's how Aunt Cece found me, huddled under the blankets, still in my clothes.

'It needs cutting, you know,' Aunt Cece said.

'I don't want to cut it!'

I was growing my hair as long as my mum's and had

ages to go so there was no way that was going to happen.

I remembered her doing my hair on a Sunday night ready for school the next morning. She'd sit behind me on the sofa, making me laugh with her funny hairdresser voice as she parted the tangles with a special comb. Then I'd do hers and we'd make toast.

'Ow!'

Aunt Cece pulled at another clump of knots and I gnawed away at my lip, biting back tears. Maybe she was trying to help, but it made me feel worse. I tried not to think how much I wished it was Mum instead of her, but as she pulled the brush through a particularly tight tangle, I couldn't stop them.

'I can cut it myself,' my aunt said. 'I do the girls' hair. Well, Kitty tells everyone she goes to a salon, but that can be our little secret.'

She brushed my hair into one hand, as if she was going to tie it up high like Kitty's. 'You'd all look the same. Wouldn't that be nice?'

'No! Never!'

She pulled her hands back as if I'd turned red hot, and I was off the chair and racing out of the house.

'Were you wearing that same outfit yesterday, young lady?' I heard her say.

Outside the air smelt like summer, thick with the scents

of flowers and sweet-smelling grass. Crickets were chirping and to me it sounded like clapping – applause for my escape from the clutches of my evil aunt and her hairbrush. Stepping out of the gloomy old house I gave them a nod of thanks.

Then a sinking feeling crept over me. I shouldn't have run off. I was supposed to be making them like me.

I shuddered. Making them like me was one thing, but nobody was going to make me look like Kitty or Fliss. I thought of the cropped pink jacket Fliss had on yesterday. and Kitty's leggings with the hearts-and-daggers pattern, and shook my head to make the images go away.

I looked across the balding gravel drive at the lands Armuth had been talking about last night. The surrounding grass and woodland stretched as far as I could see and the road disappeared off to my right. I looked up at the house to see where the face had been, but there was nothing but a boarded-up old window. I frowned. How could that be? I'd seen a face there, I was sure of it. But it wasn't the only window covered up. Uncle Vaughn was right; the house did need someone to take care of it. The pale stone was loosely patched, making the house look like it was shedding its skin and the windows that weren't boarded up had shutters hanging awkwardly with peeling broken slats. The ones nearest the ground had been repaired. One set had been painted green and below it flowers drooped from metal tubs, but the sills bled green and red where they'd rusted.

I headed across the grass towards an old tumbledown barn made of crumbling cream stone and wooden beams that looked like they were rotting. The tin roof crouched on top, as if it didn't quite fit, and around the base were wildflowers in yellows, purples and fire-engine red. I knelt to pick some and heard the giggling far too late. Kitty and Fliss appeared from nowhere and grabbed an arm each.

'We dare you to go in,' Fliss said, breathless and glancing at her sister as she pulled me towards the warped wooden door.

'Took us ages to open it,' Kitty added, pulling harder because I was digging my heels into the grass. 'Come on, we'll explore!'

'I don't want to go in,' I said. The whole barn looked dangerously close to collapse.

'Come on,' Fliss jeered. 'It's just a game.'

I shuddered. Nothing but blackness yawned from the door, and sagging cobwebs swung across the top where they'd been recently disturbed. Kitty's fingernails pinched my arm, forcing me closer.

'Tell us what happened,' Kitty said. She lowered her voice to a dangerous whisper. 'We know, really, but we want to hear your side.'

She looked at Fliss. 'After all, we're your *only* family now.' She put a hand against her mouth. 'Oops! Not supposed to mention that, are we, Fliss? Awkward!'

I wrenched my arms away and rounded on them, spitting angry but prickling with fear at the same time.

'My dad,' I said, 'my dad will . . . He'll . . .' I swallowed. 'My dad's . . .'

Fliss stepped back, her eyes wide at my threat, but Kitty stood with her hands on her hips, challenging me.

'Your dad's what? Coming to get me? I don't think so and we all know why.'

I felt like I was choking. They couldn't know; I'd never told anyone.

'It's only a joke,' Kitty said, rolling her eyes. 'God, you're so sensitive.'

'Fine,' I said, as something inside of me snapped. I'd show them sensitive.

Kitty raised her eyebrows.

'I'll do it.'

She crossed her arms.

'You're the scared ones, anyway,' I said, but my voice wobbled and they laughed. And they waited.

'Go on, then,' Fliss said, not looking at me as she concentrated on tracing a perfect circle with her foot in the bleached grass.

I turned to the dark space between the door and the

crumbling walls. The barn was falling apart. I glared at Kitty, then took a step towards the barn, then another, and then I was inside. Suddenly there was a shuffling behind me and I turned round just in time to see the door pushed shut, cutting out all the light. I heard a bolt scraping across and I knew they'd locked me in.

I could hear them laughing through the thick door – and something else. Fliss was moaning like a ghost.

'Fliss! Kitty! Let me out!'

They laughed harder.

'It's not a proper dare if you aren't locked in,' Kitty yelled.

'He'll get you,' I shouted. 'My dad'll get you and then you'll be sorry. He knows you all kidnapped me.'

I heard Kitty laugh then say, 'Oh my God, she's totally lost it,' before Fliss started her 'woooohs' again.

I waited, but Fliss's ghost noises faded and then I couldn't hear anything more outside.

Nothing.

I banged on the door. 'Let me oooooooout!'

But there was no answer. I was locked in.

Chapter Nine

I tried the door again and again, but it was useless; the bolt
held. I turned to look for another way out, but something
caught in my hair. I flinched, thinking of spiders. I hated
the horrible scuttling things, but the more I moved, the
more I got tangled. I twisted away, ripping webs from my
face and shaking the clinging strands from my fingers.
Something else brushed my neck and I shrank away,
tripped over something that scraped heavily along the
floor, and landed hard on my knees.

I screamed as loud as I could until my throat hurt. But
no one came and the thick door stayed shut. The darkness
began to press in. My knees stung where I'd scraped them
and I'd ruined my best tights.

Something ran over my hand. I jumped up and was
caught in a thin beam of light, dust motes swirling in it
like stars. I followed them like a beacon right across the

barn, hoping for another way out, and found a small hole low down the back wall. But it was no good – the hole was tiny, the size of my fist. I'd never fit through. My chest felt tight and something began to coil in the pit of my stomach, but then I remembered the rotting beams outside. It was worth a try.

I put one hand into the hole and began to scrape at the edges till I reached through to the outside. In my head I could hear Aunt Cece telling me off, saying I was damaging property. She'd never believe her precious daughters had locked me in. She'd say I was making it up and she'd tell Mrs Morrison, 'No, thanks, we don't want her,' and that would be it for me. And what about Armuth and Herman? It was their barn and I didn't want to mess it up. Thinking about that made my chest tight. Thinking about living with Kitty and Fliss made it worse. I thought about Kitty saying my clothes stank and Fliss giggling as they locked me in. They were mean, but it was better than the kids' home – a hundred times better. There were only two of them for a start and I did know them, sort of. Of course, I'd have to look at their pink and sparkly outfits every day, which would be a cruel and terrible torture, but I'd cope.

As I pulled at the plaster, I tried to think up an excuse for damaging the wall that wouldn't get me into trouble. It crumbled quickly. Huge clumps came away one after the other and in seconds I was able to use both hands. But I must have disturbed something, because the rotten beam above my head cracked and split, tipping a thousand woodlice into my lap.

I leapt back, shaking off as many as I could. My skin prickled as if they were crawling inside it, but I had to keep going. I reached back into the hole, making it wider, trying to ignore the bugs until it was big enough to crawl through. I lay down on my front. The woodlice were frantic now they were out in the light. They scrabbled across my bare skin where my shirt had ridden up as I pulled myself through. I screwed up my face, holding my breath so they wouldn't get in my mouth or eyes. Then I dug my hands into the grass to pull my legs through and I was out in the sunlight and the warm, soupy air. I stood up, still shaking woodlice off as the crickets chirped more applause. I heard the gentle *thwock* of a bat on a ball, then I heard them.

'She's escaped! Our prisoner's escaped!'

Kitty was already running towards me.

'Get her!'

I didn't stop to think. I raced round the back of the barn, still shedding bugs.

'Come on, Fliss!'

I ran through an overgrown field and jumped over an abandoned piece of machinery left to rust in the long grass. But I had to change direction. Kitty won prizes at her school for running and I was not going back into that barn or anywhere else.

I decided she wouldn't want to get caught and turned towards the house. My fingers skimmed the wall to stop myself slipping as I skidded along the gravel. As I reached the back door I chanced a quick look back. Fliss had fallen way behind, but Kitty was close. Too close.

As I leapt over the doorstep into the house, tore through the kitchen, straight past the library and into the main hall, I glimpsed my aunt and uncle in the small salon.

'Whoever's making that godawful racket will stop it, right now!' Aunt Cece's voice rang out followed by the clash of a cup into a saucer. I slid to a stop then started towards my side of the house, but then I heard the kitchen door slam. Kitty was coming. Mutterings about 'trying to have a cup of decent tea' were coming from the salon on my left. My room was on the right and close, but it was too easy for Kitty to find. I raced back to the main hall, my trainers skidding on the waxed floor, but this time there was someone standing at the bottom of the staircase. Herman.

He stood at least twice my height and loomed over me as I wobbled to a stop just short of barging into him. He stared down his long nose as I held my breath and waited to be told off, already flipping through three potential excuses. Instead, his gaze shifted to something behind me. I turned to look.

Kitty!

I hopped nervously from foot to foot. Then, to my complete surprise, Herman moved aside to let me upstairs.

Upstairs was out of bounds. I couldn't believe it, but I was already racing up two stairs at a time as Kitty rattled down the hallway. I reached the first-floor balcony and heard her slowing down, but not stopping. I'd have to go further. On the second floor I stopped to catch my breath, listening to both cousins at the foot of the stairs.

'We should leave her,' Fliss said, panting. 'I don't want to go up there. Armuth said.'

'No,' Kitty said, 'we have to. Come on! It's the only way she could have gone.'

'But what about Mum?' Fliss said.

While they argued I crept up to the third floor. The landing split left and right with doors along each side and a dim, gloomy light seeping through the broken shutters.

I rattled door handles, one after another, hearing two sets of footsteps on the stairs getting closer and closer, but every door was locked. I could hear puffing and could swear I felt their hot breath on my neck. I reached for the last door at the very end of the corridor, twisted the handle and . . . it opened!

I flew into the room then shut the door quietly behind me and leant against it.

The room smelt musty and stale. The dust I'd disturbed began to crawl up my nose. I pinched it, but the tickling got worse and worse.

Kitty and Fliss were prowling along the third floor. They were trying door handles and finding each one locked, just like I had. I gripped mine, hoping that if I held on tightly enough, I could make them think this one was locked too. But the urge to sneeze was getting worse and worse. I couldn't stop it coming. I squeezed my eyes tight, but it was no good.

'*Achoo.*'

I pressed my ear to the door and heard them right outside. Had they heard me? I held my breath and listened.

'Six, seven, eight,' Fliss said. 'They're all locked.'

'She must have gone down another way,' Kitty said. 'Come on.'

I heard their footsteps fade. I sighed and sagged against the door. After a few seconds I felt about for a light, but there was nothing on the wall by the door. Noticing a chink of light across the room, I walked over to the window and pulled back the heavy curtain. But as light flooded the room through the broken boards, so did a swirling grey cloud of dust. I doubled over, coughing and sneezing, my eyes streaming. The dust began to settle.

Then there was a sneeze behind me.

I froze.

I turned to the door but it was shut. No one had come in. I looked round the room at the bulging furniture shapes under sheets, and smudges across the floor where my footprints had disturbed the carpet of dust. Nothing looked out of place.

The back of my neck began to prickle. I thought of the face at the window last night and suddenly, out of the corner of my eye, something moved on the far wall.

A mirror peeked out from under a greying cloth. It reflected half of me, ripped tights and all. Suddenly the mirror bulged like those ones at fairs that make you taller or fatter. Gasping, I pulled the heavy cloth away.

The mirror was huge, easily twice the size of me. It had a bevelled edge running around its octagonal shape and silver splotches spreading across it like a pretty mould. Now I was up close I looked blurry, as if my edges were smudged. I ran my hand over it and thick, fluffy grey clumps of dust coated my fingers. The silvered splotches didn't budge even when I tried to scrape some with my nail. I was thinking about writing my name in the dust when the mirror bulged again. The bulges settled into thick waves rippling across the surface until I couldn't see myself in it any more. But I could see something else.

The mirror was now full of flickering light, with twenty, maybe thirty candles of all different shapes and sizes.

I spun round, but there was nothing behind me but a bare wall with wallpaper dripping to the floor. It was the same old dusty room it was five minutes ago. But the mirror was showing me another room!

Suddenly something flickered at the edge of my vision. I turned back to the mirror, and gasped.

A boy was standing right in the middle.

For a second we stared at each other. Then he screamed.

Chapter Ten

I screamed too.

Then he shouted something at me in French and I was so surprised I stopped.

He was a pale boy, tall with floppy dark blond hair that came down to his chin. He seemed to be wearing a kind of a long nightshirt with small holes in it. He looked older than me and kind of dirty, as if he didn't wash, like some of the kids back in the home.

'*Va t'en!*' he said. He stumbled back unsteadily, waving me away.

'Hey!' I said, holding my nose because a smell of stale and sour things poured out of the mirror. The boy retreated further back until his legs hit the frame of his bed. Then he began to hiss at me, his eyes darting left and right.

'I'm not going to hurt you or anything,' I said, reaching out. 'I'm Angela.'

To my horror and shock and complete surprise my hand disappeared into the mirror towards him. It felt like I'd dipped myself into a bowl of cold squishy air.

'Go. Go away!' he shouted. 'It's not safe!'

I didn't move at first, my mouth hanging open now the boy had spoken English, and between staring at him and at my hand stuck half in, half out of a mirror into a whole other room, I was trying to make sense of it all.

'Go!'

The mirror bulged. My arm felt squashed and pushed as if it was a blister the mirror was trying to dislodge. I pulled it back, and opened and closed my hand, making sure everything still worked. Then I looked up. The boy was still staring. He took a step back and his foot nudged one of the candles. The mirror bulged once more. The candle began to tip over. I pointed to it and managed to squeak out, 'Wait, look!' before the mirror rippled, then gave a *thunk* as it set hard. All I could see was my own reflection. For a second I stood there staring, my shoulders heaving, my eyes wide and my hair all over the place. Then I grabbed the edge of the mirror and pressed a hand against it. I felt sick. What if the boy hadn't seen the candle? What if it fell and there was a fire? But the mirror stayed solid and only showed my face, my hand. I let go.

I had to get help.

I ran out into the corridor and bumped straight into Kitty and Fliss.

'Ha!' Kitty shouted, lunging for me. 'Where were you hiding? We tried all the doors.'

'You're not supposed to go off on your own,' Fliss said, 'and you're not allowed up here.' She looked at Kitty. 'We'll tell Mum, won't we?'

But Kitty was busy trying to grab me and I was making it difficult because I was hopping about.

'Wait,' I said, trying to catch a breath. 'You've got to come. You've got to help him!'

'What?' Kitty said, trying to hold on to my sleeve. 'Is it a game? Because it's so not funny.'

She pinched my arm, but I shook her off.

'Where were you hiding?' she said. 'Tell me!'

I ignored her.

'Listen. There's a fire!' I swallowed. 'A candle fell. And there's a boy. You have to come quickly!'

Kitty and Fliss shared a look.

'A boy?' said Fliss, wrinkling her nose.

'A boy!' said Kitty, her eyes lighting up.

I ran back to the room with the mirror, but they didn't follow. I knew I sounded crazy. I thought about what I'd shouted in the barn, about my dad coming to rescue me, and realised they thought I was making this up too. My cheeks felt red hot, but this was important.

'Come on,' I said, pleading. 'We've got to help him!'

They shared another look and after a pause, Fliss shrugged her shoulders and Kitty shook her head, but they came.

'At least we know where her hiding place is,' Kitty said as she walked in.

I was already pushing at the mirror.

'This place is gross,' Fliss said, brushing specks of dust from her skirt. Kitty was looking round with her nose in the air.

I stood in front of the mirror and put my hand against it. Nothing. I tried again, but my hand wouldn't go through.

'Help me!' I shouted and with a long sigh, Kitty smoothed her ponytail and sauntered over. Fliss followed and stood next to me with Kitty on her other side, but no amount of pushing and shoving would make the mirror do anything. Kitty let go first and Fliss followed seconds after. I carried on pushing, but it was useless. I slumped against it.

'So, where's this boy, then?' Kitty said. 'Who is he, your boyfriend?'

Fliss giggled.

'No,' I said, giving her my best sarcastic smile, 'I saw . . .'

But now they were there with me and the mirror was just being a mirror, I began to wonder what I'd seen. Kitty raised her eyebrows.

'There was a boy in the mirror,' I said, taking a deep breath, 'and candles – and one of them fell.'

I stopped because Kitty was shaking her head again and Fliss had looked away.

'It's true,' I said. 'I saw it. I saw him!'

Kitty toyed with the edge of a dustsheet next to her.

'Like there'd be a boy here,' she said, 'and he'd be interested in you.' She gave a giggle. 'I mean, no offence.'

I narrowed my eyes. 'There was. There was a boy,' I said. 'And, for your information, there were tons of boys at the home and they all liked me.'

Kitty spat out a laugh. 'Oh. My. God. Of course they did. It must have been your adorable home-made clothes that made them so keen.'

She pulled at the sheet and we all jumped as something leapt off an empty bookshelf. Kitty squealed, then tutted as we watched a rusted yellow-and-red striped spinning top roll in tight, noisy circles on the floor.

'We don't want to play your stupid games,' she said. 'This room is boring. Stay if you like.'

'. . . with your boyfriend,' Fliss said quietly and they laughed.

'Wait!'

I sneezed then, thanks to the dust still swirling, three times. Kitty and Fliss both shrieked with as much drama as possible, holding their noses and covering their mouths as if I was contagious. They raced out the room, slamming the door and stirring up more dust, which set me off sneezing again.

'It's true!' I shouted, but they were gone. I knew if there'd been a key they'd have locked me in as well. Instead, their footsteps faded. I turned back to the mirror, reached out and gave the surface one last half-hearted shove, but nothing happened.

I thought about the face at the window last night, the face with the fire behind it. It had to be the boy with all those candles, in the room behind the mirror. But what was he doing there and what if the candle sent the whole place up in flames? I felt sick.

I grabbed the mirror and scratched at the surface till my hands stung, but it didn't change at all. I watched a bee buzz uselessly against the shut window, and felt just like it.

Armuth had said there was nothing up here so the boy had to be hiding. Maybe he was trapped. Maybe he'd been looking out the window for help. Well, he was going to need more help than Kitty and Fliss, and that meant telling someone – Armuth, Herman, Uncle Vaughn or, worst case scenario, Aunt Cece.

I tried to brush as much dirt and dust from the barn and the room off me as possible as I ran into the corridor and down the stairs, but there was no hiding the mess

I was in. I'd have to change before I went looking for anyone, but it was too late. Aunt Cece was already waiting for me at the bottom of the stairs and she did not look happy.

Chapter Eleven

'Look at you,' Aunt Cece said as I shuffled slowly down the stairs towards her. 'Upstairs is out of bounds. Were we not clear about that?' She looked over her shoulder then back at me. 'Was *I* not clear?'

Aunt Cece was a very skinny woman and her whole body seemed to vibrate as she waited for me to answer.

'I found a boy.'

'What?' She put up her hand to stop whatever I was going to say next, but I carried on.

'I did, I really did, and I think he's in trouble.'

At this she looked behind her again, leant forward, grabbed my shoulder and pulled me down the hallway, venting her anger with each stomp of her feet.

'You're covered in dirt and worse.'

Stomp.

'What if Armuth had seen you upstairs?'

Stomp.

'You're a guest in this house.'

Stomp.

'Not just our guest, but her guest and you behave like this, making up stories and leading my girls astray.'

Stomp.

'You should try harder, Angela.'

Stomp.

'If you want a home.'

Stomp, stomp, stomp.

I tuned her out and didn't resist. She'd never be able to hear anything bad about her girls, my perfect cousins.

She marched me into the small downstairs bathroom I shared with Armuth. It was an odd room dwarfed by a huge tub, with dark wood on the walls instead of wallpaper. Wood was everywhere. You even had to lift a panel on a bench to find the toilet. She leant over the bath and turned on the taps, every gesture pointy and precise, as she fussed with soaps and rearranged bottles of bath salts.

'I'm sure that nice Mrs Morrison did all she could,' she said, 'but you have to stop making up stories. Boys upstairs indeed.'

'Not boys,' I said. 'One boy.'

She looked at me as if I was crazy then pointed at the bath. 'And don't think about getting out until I get back, young lady.'

With that she shut the door and I was left alone. The bath seemed to take forever to fill so I got in when the water was about halfway only for her to storm back in carrying a pile of clothes. I hunched over, trying to cover as much of me with bubbles as I could. I held the top of my right arm with my left, covering my scar.

'You can wear some of Fliss's old things,' she said. Then, misunderstanding my look of horror, said, 'Don't worry, I'll buy her something new. I just cannot bear seeing you walk around like some sort of mix and match urchin.'

My jaw tightened. I bit my lip and turned away. I'd made those clothes myself. I made all the clothes I had with me from leftovers they'd given me at the home. My clothes were one of a kind. Vintage, even. She had no right to say they were rubbish.

'I've put your towel here,' she continued, popping it onto a rail made out of more dark wood. 'It's lucky Armuth had spares.'

She leant over and began to wash my hair, telling me it was high time it was cleaned properly. I flinched and her voice softened.

'You'd have your own towels if you lived with us,' she said, 'and we could get you some new clothes too, but you need to start fitting in.' She paused. 'No stories.'

'It's true!' I said, turning in protest, but she gripped my

head, working the shampoo in with her long, polished nails.

'You do want to stay with us, don't you? You don't want to have to go to a new home? Mrs Morrison told me everything; about the fights, and your running away all the time. Not to mention the stories you told. And if that's how you behave . . . well, who wants to live with that? You have to start thinking about the future.'

'I don't care,' I mumbled under my breath, and that was the truth. Sort of. Being away from it, I realised I really didn't want to go back to the kids' home or to a new kids' home, but I didn't want to live with the horror that was my aunt, uncle and cousins either. My chest felt tight. I didn't want to go anywhere except to my own home, but that was the last place I could go now. I had no choice. I'd have to try harder with my aunt. Something caught in the back of my throat and my eyes stung. Shampoo slid down my face.

Aunt Cece finished rinsing my hair and stood up. I turned away from her, sniffing.

She flapped her arms at the pile of clothes she'd left me and when I didn't say anything, she scooped up my dirty clothes and moved to the door.

'No, they're mine! Leave them alone.'

She looked just like Kitty as she slowly shook her head. 'Angela, they need to be washed.' She paused.

I looked away.

'I've decided this is going to be a lovely holiday, Angela,' she said, her voice like a thick oil, 'and we could be one big happy family.'

It was totally creepy. I said nothing and kept my back to her.

'Now, you show me some manners and some responsibility, and everything will work out perfectly,' she said, and walked out.

I turned and stared at the open door with a hot, stinging feeling in my chest. It filled my ribcage till there was nowhere else for it to go. I felt like I might explode.

She wanted me to take responsibility, but that was a joke because I knew all about that. Like when Mrs Morrison said what happened with my family wasn't my fault, when I knew it was. I shivered.

And Aunt Cece thought we could be a happy family. I snorted. Yeah, right. A fake family with pink sparkly jackets, phony smiles and perfectly brushed hair.

The bath water was cold. I got out and pulled the door shut, then reached for the clothes she'd left. I sighed. Of course they were all pink.

I shrugged on a T-shirt covered with felt strawberries, a pair of dark pink leggings and a white cardigan embroidered with pink and red roses. It had a fake fur collar, which I unhooked. I stared at myself in the mirror. It was like pink had thrown up all over me.

I thought about cutting out the T-shirt strawberries and sewing them onto my old jeans, then I remembered I didn't have those jeans any more. It was like a punch in the stomach. I looked at the bare collar, trying to rack my brains for some way I could make the outfit less hideous. Then I thought of the wardrobe in my bedroom. There might be something there, and the clothes looked like they might fit me . . .

I put my hand to my mouth. They had to be his clothes, the boy upstairs! They were just the right size for him, and looked a bit old-fashioned, like he did. So why were they down here when he was upstairs? And if he had clothes here, did that mean Herman and Armuth knew he was up there?

I flung my towel over the rail and hopped back to my bedroom on tiptoes because Aunt Cece had taken my trainers as well as my clothes. The floor was like ice. Once inside I delved through the wardrobe. I pulled out a shirt that looked almost exactly like the one the boy had been wearing, held it up against me, then out in front of me. I frowned. No, it wasn't just similar, it was *exactly* the same. It had the round open collar and two ties across the neck. I ran a hand over the jagged hem, the same snags and holes I'd seen on him. Now I knew these clothes were definitely his. But how could they be? I'd seen him wearing this exact shirt earlier when I was upstairs. It didn't make sense.

The dinner bell trilled.

I hung his shirt back up and quickly stuffed on a pair of socks. As the bell rang again I raced to the kitchen. I was going to find out exactly who this boy was.

Chapter Twelve

I was the last to arrive, again, so I took the same seat next to Herman, keeping well away from Aunt Cece. He raised a bushy eyebrow at all the pink and I shrugged. Kitty giggled, but Fliss crossed her arms and wouldn't look at me. Obviously she didn't want me to have her clothes, which was fine by me; I didn't want them, either. I tugged at the neck of the cardigan. It itched now I'd taken the collar off.

'There are many tales told about the house, but for over a hundred years there has been one tale that has haunted the family.'

Armuth hadn't taken a breath since I came in as she set up her story and her words drew my attention as I helped myself to the plate of cold chicken with something grey and slimy swimming in a bowl. I took a small bit because I was starving, but it turned out to be lettuce, peas, herbs and butter, and it was really tasty. I took another scoop and another, noticing my cousins hadn't bothered to try it at all.

'It was a young boy we believe that cursed the house.'

Fliss spat bits of chicken across the table and Kitty burst into giggles. Aunt Cece glared down at her plate, her eyes blinking triple time.

'Now now, girls,' Uncle Vaughn said, trying to hide a smile and not really managing it. But they were hysterical. Fliss was laughing so much she couldn't speak, but Kitty managed to bark out a few words.

'It. Must. Be. Angela's. Boyfriend.'

They both dissolved, Kitty hanging off her chair and Fliss so slumped she'd almost disappeared under the table.

'Girls!'

Aunt Cece pulled Fliss up by her top, but neither she nor Kitty stopped laughing. Something nudged my foot so I peered under the table. It was a small pink torch. It must have fallen out of Fliss's pocket as she was hauled up. I leant down as if I was scratching my ankle, scooped it into my sleeve and sat back all in about five seconds. No one had seen a thing.

Armuth was waving at my aunt. 'No matter, Cece. If they do not want to hear about the ghost then I will not speak another word.'

Kitty and Fliss immediately stopped giggling and sat

up straight. Kitty flashed a look at me and I held my breath.

Armuth nodded at them. 'He died. It was so tragic. They say he disappeared somewhere in the house and was never seen again.'

There was silence round the table.

I gulped. The boy upstairs – was he a ghost?

'Some say he walks the house at night,' she said, looking at each of us in turn.

I sat totally still, thinking about the footsteps I'd heard, almost numb.

Aunt Cece was twitching though. She cleared her throat and arranged her face into a smile. 'Armuth, I'm not sure this is appropriate.'

But she needn't have worried because my cousins chose that moment to burst into giggles again. Kitty pointed at me while Fliss was busy holding her sides.

'It *is* Angela's boyfriend,' Kitty said.

Fliss nodded, unable to speak.

'Angela's seen him,' Kitty said to the table between hiccups, before adding, 'They're in love.'

Aunt Cece frowned. 'What did I say?' she said through her teeth.

'Oh come on,' Uncle Vaughn said, 'they're just having a bit of fun.'

Aunt Cece gave him the full force of a scowl she'd

probably meant for me, but when Armuth caught her eye she forced it into a polite smile and pretended to brush a hair from her face.

'Why don't you make him one of your little outfits?' Kitty said, looking at my new pink ensemble. 'You usually wear clothes people probably died in and he's a ghost. It's totally adorable. You're perfect for each other.'

That set them off again.

This time the adults smiled indulgently at each other, but I was seething. I stood up, knocking my chair back.

'I've seen the boy; I've seen him twice and I'm not lying.'

I pushed the kitchen door open and stormed out. There was a boy. He wasn't some ghost story Armuth and Herman had made up to scare us.

I pulled out Fliss's torch. Pockets of laughter bubbled from the kitchen. It burnt my cheeks. Suddenly I wanted my old clothes back so much I felt like ripping Fliss's off me. I ran to my room, clutching the torch so tightly the plastic cracked.

I'd prove it; I'd prove I saw the boy. I had to show them I wasn't making it up.

I waited just inside my bedroom door for what seemed like forever, flicking Fliss's torch on and off again. After a while I noticed it had grown really dark. I pressed my ear to the door and eventually I heard the kitchen door bang and footsteps fading down the hallway. That had to be Armuth and Herman, so the others must have gone back to the guesthouse already. I counted to thirty. Then I set off to find him.

Chapter Thirteen

I padded along the hallway in my socked feet. Moonlight peeped through the warped and broken shutters. I veered away from the suit of armour, keeping it in the corner of my eye in case it decided to lunge. Then I was standing at the bottom of the huge staircase. It seemed to disappear up into nothing.

I thought about Aunt Cece and what she'd do if she caught me after her warning. It would be game over, no stupid happy family. I took a deep breath and thought about turning back, but then I looked off to the right, where the kitchen door would be, and remembered them all laughing at me. That decided it. I was going.

I placed one foot on the first step but it creaked so loudly and for so long that I was sure everyone had to have heard. I froze and listened out for anything other than my own heartbeat. I waited to be caught, but no one came.

I took a deep breath, but all I could hear was wind rattling through loose shutters. Without another thought I ran up to the first, second, then third floor.

At the top I switched on the torch and made my way to the mirror room. The door handle was squeaky so I slipped in and quickly shut the door behind me, swinging the torch beam around the black. But where the mirror should have been was a pair of shining eyes floating in the dark.

I screamed, let go of the torch, then dropped to the floor scrabbling for it. But it must have rolled out of my reach – my fingers only found dust. Remembering the eyes, I snatched my hands back. Armuth was right. There was a ghost – and he was right here.

I wriggled backwards, feeling for the door. There was a shuffling noise in front of me and I couldn't help it. I looked.

The eyes hung in mid-air. I screamed again.

But the moon crept from behind a cloud and shone in-between the curtains I'd left open earlier, and I saw now that the eyes had a face around them, and a body, and a dress. No, not dress, a nightshirt. I gulped. The boy in the mirror was staring straight at me.

He reached towards me.

'No!' I gasped in fright, groping for the door handle.

The boy dropped his arms and stepped closer, revealing

flickering lights illuminating him from behind. His floppy hair shone round his face like a halo and he began to look more solid, more real.

Wait! I realised why. I wasn't looking at him through the mirror any more – the mirror had moved, actually moved! It rested against the wall about a metre from where it had been, as if it had been pushed aside. And behind it was an open doorway that led into a whole other room; a dark room that looked like it was swaying from all the candlelight bobbing up and down its walls.

I let go of my door and stood up. The boy was staring at me from the doorway with his head cocked to one side and his arm twitching towards me, and I wondered if he'd been wanting to help me up, not scare me half to death.

'*Cette porte était verrouillée,*' he said, gesturing to the right of the mirror.

I shook my head. 'I don't understand,' I said.

His eyes widened. 'There is a door here,' he said. 'It was locked. It has always been locked. How did you open it?'

My voice seemed to have disappeared suddenly. He was speaking English. Also, he was actually here. And talking to me.

When I didn't answer, his mouth twisted. 'Who are you?' he said. 'Where did you come from?' He paused. 'Are you a ghost?'

My words faltered, then I drew myself up as tall as I could. 'I'm Angela,' I said, pretending to brush dust off me, pretending I hadn't just completely freaked out, screamed like a baby and scrabbled on the floor like a complete idiot. 'I didn't know there was a door here. There was a mirror in front of it, and no, obviously I'm not a ghost.'

He shook his head as if he didn't believe me.

'I'm here on holiday with my . . .' I paused. ' . . .with my parents. We're having a brilliant time.' I folded my arms across my chest. 'We'll probably buy this house because we have tons of money so you should tell me who you are and why you're hiding up here in a secret room.'

He raised his eyebrows, but before he could answer I remembered the mirror bulging. I'd seen him *through* the mirror, not behind it! I had another question.

'Wait. Are *you* a ghost?'

He looked at me sideways, frowned and opened his mouth as if he was about to yell again. I winced, but he didn't shout. Instead he looked over his shoulder, then back at me before speaking.

'I'm Julien,' he said, but that was all he managed before a hacking cough ripped through his body. He bent over, clutching his right side and waved me away as he stumbled back into his room and onto his bed.

The silvered splotches on the mirror rippled as I peered through his doorway after him. It was just as stuffy as before and full of candles, the hot little flames making everything shimmer and sway. It was a small room with thick roof beams meeting in a triangle point above, like in an attic, with a set of heavy curtains to the left and right. The ones on the right weren't quite pulled together and behind them were wooden boards nailed across a window.

The candle I'd seen fall over had been righted and re-lit, one more to add to what seemed like hundreds. They made my eyes swim and filled my head with smoke, just like my nightmare.

Julien's coughing brought me back. There was a jug of water on a table next to his bed. Before I could change my mind, I strode in and poured him a glass. He sipped it with shaking hands. His cough turned into a wheeze. It sounded eerie, as if something was rattling around in his chest.

'*Je suis désolé,*' he said. Then, 'I mean, I'm sorry – for shouting at you, before.'

I shrugged.

'And I'm sorry you've come so close.' He pulled a faded quilt up to his chin. 'You should leave while you still can.'

'Why?' I said, glancing at the doorway to check the mirror hadn't swung back. It hadn't. From here, a door opened inwards, and beyond led directly to the third-floor room, but the air seemed to ripple where I'd come from, like above tarmac on a hot day. I could see the peeling wallpaper through the doorway, but it was blurry. A shiver ran up my spine. I turned round to the boy.

'What do you mean, "while I still can"?'

'I'm sick,' he said, between sips of water. 'You can't stay here.'

He coughed so hard then that he let go of his glass. I caught it just in time. It felt warm and clammy. Beads of sweat sprouted across his forehead and he'd begun to shake. I took a step backwards. He didn't look well, but as Mrs Morrison used to say, no one ever died from coughing or sneezing.

He coughed again but this time he couldn't seem to stop. I put the glass down and reached out to pat him on the back, but he sprang away from me as if I was contagious. I snatched my hand back.

His face grew hard. He picked up the nearest candle and brandished it at me. 'If you stay here, you'll die.'

His eyes blazed as if he were mad. His nostrils flared, his mouth distorted. The flame in his hand seemed drawn towards me, like it was hungry. I backed away, stumbling until I felt the doorframe in my hands. I stepped through and the boy's door slammed shut, plunging me into darkness. I heard a lock click, then, before I could take a breath, the mirror sliced across the wall, cutting between me and the door as quick as a guillotine.

It was pitch black. I remembered the torch, but I was shaking too much to look for it. I didn't care who the boy was any more. I'd only tried to help, but he didn't want any. He didn't want anything to do with me.

I lurched into the corridor and raced down the stairs to the second floor, then to the first, not caring if I was too loud. I only wanted to be as far away from him and the mirror as possible. My heart beat triple time. My socked feet slid along the wooden floor. I was so intent on getting away that I didn't notice I was about to bump into someone, not until they were right there in front of me.

Chapter Fourteen

'Herman!'

Clouds hurried past a window left open, its shutters drawn back. The moon lit up a very tall, looming and stern-looking Herman.

I felt a scream in the back of my throat and wrapped my hands round my mouth to stop it escaping. I waited to be shouted at. If he told Aunt Cece, that was it for me, but Herman didn't say a word.

He gave me a long, quizzical look down his nose, his heavy eyebrows bunching in the middle. Then he put a finger to his lips and beckoned for me to follow him downstairs.

'I didn't mean to,' I said, babbling. 'I got lost. I needed the bathroom.'

That sounded lame even to me, and I wasn't even sure he understood English, but when he didn't say anything, I couldn't help myself.

'There's a boy up there. There really is. I'm not lying.'

Herman shook his head and carried on down the stairs. So he did understand. I could have kicked myself. Now I was in even more trouble.

But when we reached the bottom, he didn't lead me towards the guesthouse or Armuth's room. Instead he took me to the kitchen. The door had been propped open and inside it was still cosy and warm from dinner. Herman gestured to the fridge. It was a massive old-fashioned one with a sticking door, but once I'd opened it, he pointed to the milk, which I took out, then to a box on a wooden shelf above the range. I closed the fridge then had to stand on a chair to reach the shelf which, given Herman was so tall seemed a bit unnecessary, but he hadn't said anything about me being upstairs, so I didn't say anything either.

Inside the box was a thick block of chocolate wrapped in paper and foil. Herman pointed to the row of copper saucepans hanging in order of size above my head. I chose a small pan, placed it on the range and added milk, a little at first then more at Herman's nods. I added a huge chunk of the chocolate, and as the block melted into a gooey paste I felt my shoulders relax. When the mix was about to bubble I checked with Herman and took it off the stove, poured it into two cups and offered him the first. He shook his head, pointing to me then to the cups again. I grinned.

The hot chocolate was amazing, thick as treacle and rich without being sickly. I sat with my back to the stove, toasty warm, the copper pans turning and twinkling. In the quiet I felt a tightness in me start to loosen. When I'd finished both cups I washed them up. Herman had moved to the dresser where stacks of crinkly old papers had been spread out with a pen resting next on top. I reached past him to hang the cups back on their hooks and peered at them.

The one on the top looked like a complicated document, something legal, perhaps. It was something to do with the house anyway because it had *Maison de Noyer* typed at the top. I remembered Armuth saying they were going to have to sell. She'd said something about it being because of Herman, but I couldn't remember why now.

Herman studied the papers. His face was drawn and sad.

'Herman?'

He didn't stir from the papers. I looked closer at the page he was reading and something caught my eye. It looked like my dad's name, but surely it couldn't be. I glanced at Herman, but he hadn't noticed I was looking. I peered closer at the papers and saw it *was* my dad's name. But that was impossible. I stared at the other words, but apart from his name the rest was all in French. My neck prickled and my stomach felt tight. I had to know why his name was on these old papers. I'd never been to this house before and neither had my dad, as far as I knew.

'Herman?' I said, louder this time, but he didn't respond.

'Herman? Why is my dad's name here?' I said, but it was as if he hadn't heard me at all. He continued to stare at the papers, then, he turned to me, one hand to his throat. He shook his head. I gasped. His throat! Was that why he didn't speak? Was that why he couldn't help Armuth with the house? But before I could ask, or say sorry, or anything at all, Herman walked out of the kitchen.

'Wait!' I said, but he'd melted into the darkness.

I followed him out then turned back to look at my dad's name. Suddenly I wanted that piece of paper more than anything. I put out my hand, but there was a noise. I froze. The ceiling above my head began to creak. The footsteps were back.

I swallowed and thought of the boy. Had the mirror moved again? Had he left his room? I could feel the shimmering heat of the candles, see him brandish one at me. I felt the snapping jaw of the mirror, the slam of the door. Or was it Armuth coming back, or ten times worse, Aunt Cece?

There was a creak, then another and another. They were getting closer and closer. Someone was coming this way and if it wasn't Herman I was in big trouble. Abandoning the papers, I fled to my room.

Chapter Fifteen

The footsteps chased me to my room then stopped above my head, just like last time. I crawled into the tangle of blankets and must've fallen asleep, because when I opened my eyes again I was still dressed in Fliss's clothes. It was morning and my first thought was about the papers. I itched to get them.

Outside my bedroom the shutters were closed so I thought I must be the only one up, but then I heard it.

'Angela.'

I froze.

'Angela . . . Angela . . . Angela,' echoed along the hallway.

Then another voice I recognised joined in and I realised it was my aunt and uncle. I crept out and hid behind the suit of armour, but because they were whispering, I couldn't quite hear what they were saying. I definitely heard Aunt Cece say, 'It's a potential goldmine.' Then my ears pricked as she added, 'And she won't find out if you stick to the plan.'

Uncle Vaughn said something I couldn't make out, then Aunt Cece raised her voice.

'You've spent enough already. You promised, remember? We're almost there. She'll sign, I know it.'

My foot shifted, making the suit squeak.

'Who's there? Angela?'

I was totally busted.

Aunt Cece strode towards me so I slipped out from behind the suit, giving it a dirty look.

'Why are you sneaking around? Were you listening? It's bad manners to eavesdrop.'

Before I could say I wasn't sneaking, listening or eavesdropping (fingers crossed behind my back) she put her hand to her forehead like she had a headache.

I noticed Uncle Vaughn had taken the opportunity to disappear.

'We've had breakfast,' Aunt Cece said, frowning now she'd noticed he wasn't where she'd left him. 'You'll have to miss yours.'

She coughed delicately and turned to me, so I stopped. 'We're going out for the day, and night; the four, I mean, five of us.' She gave me a sickly sweet smile. 'To stay with relatives,' she said.

I waited.

'Family, you know?'

Ouch. Ouch. Ouch.

'That'll be nice, won't it?' The corners of her mouth had lifted so high her eyes sunk into her cheeks.

Actually, it sounded awful, but I couldn't say that, not if I wanted them to like me. I wished they didn't want to take me with them. I wished I could stay with Armuth and Herman instead.

That was it! I felt a smile coming.

I coughed, then forced out a couple of fake sneezes.

Aunt Cece skipped backwards so fast she looked like an insect doing a dance. I began to laugh then covered my mouth with my hand and coughed over and over again.

'I don't think I'm very well,' I said.

Aunt Cece wrung her hands like she was washing them. I thought of the boy last night, and what he'd said to me about being sick.

'It might be catching.' I took a step towards her and she flinched, waving her hand at me.

'Well, perhaps it's best you stay here. Because of your . . . cold.'

I waited. This was too easy.

'Vaughn's aunt is old and we can't risk her getting sick . . . her or the girls.' She looked behind her. 'Look, stay here, but you do exactly what Armuth says.' She wafted a hand at me again. 'And don't say a word, not one word.'

I shrugged my shoulders. 'About what?'

'About anything,' she snapped. Then she shut her eyes and took a breath before opening them again; that weird smile playing across her lips. 'Armuth is a busy lady. She won't want to hear about you . . . or anything.'

She reached out and patted me on the shoulder like I was a pet that might bite. This was definitely too easy. I felt a squeeze in my stomach. Aunt Cece hadn't wanted me to go with them. Not really.

'Now you keep quiet and be well-behaved, and we'll be back tomorrow.'

Well this was perfect for me. I'd be rid of my cousins and my aunt and uncle, even if it was only for one day. And I knew exactly what I wanted to do with that time. I thought about Herman and the papers. I was going to find out why my dad's name was on them.

Just as I was thinking about him, Herman appeared outside the kitchen. He must have heard everything. I grinned at him, but he raised one large beetled eyebrow so high I made an effort to look disappointed about not going with them, for Aunt Cece's benefit.

'Do we have a deal?' she asked, but I was saved from having to answer by my cousins careering out of the kitchen.

'Shopping!' Kitty yelled, twirling round and round.

Fliss stopped when she saw me, looked me up and down and announced, 'I'm getting a whole new outfit now, anyway,' before following her sister with giant skips.

I ignored them both. It wasn't as if I even wanted Fliss's clothes. It wasn't as if I wanted any new ones either. What I wanted was my old clothes back. I wanted everything back, exactly the way it was.

I followed them all to the front door and watched them drive away. It was already warm outside, the air thick like soup and the crickets clapping away in the overgrown grass. I waited till the car had disappeared and the dust from the road had settled, then let out a long, slow breath I didn't know I'd been holding in.

'You'll entertain yourself, yes?'

I jumped. Armuth was standing right behind me.

'Yes, yes,' I said.

Her little eyes seemed to flit over me and then away again. I thought about asking her about the papers, about my dad's name and even about the boy upstairs then I remembered what Aunt Cece had said about not bothering her. I gave what I hoped was an innocent-looking smile. She opened her mouth as if she was going to say something, then looked over my shoulder at the driveway. Her brow furrowed, she gave me a small smile, a gentle pat on my arm, then turned on her squeaky shoes and headed back to the kitchen shaking her head. I followed her, ready to put my plan in action, but when I checked the dresser, the papers were gone.

I frowned, then I noticed the drawers underneath. Maybe the papers had been tidied away. I reached for the latticed doors just as Armuth dumped a heavy bowl onto the table. I shoved my hands behind my back as she eyed the dresser, then me, then the dresser again. When she looked back I met her stare until my eyes started to water then she shook her head. As I tiptoed out, I heard her sigh.

I scuffed my feet along the corridor then peered into the small salon. No Herman. I worked my way round the whole of the ground floor looking for him, checking every room that wasn't locked, before finding myself back in front of the closed kitchen door, but he was nowhere to be seen.

'Herman?' I whispered, then jumped as behind me Armuth thumped something else onto the kitchen table, then another thing and then something that sounded even heavier. It sort of sounded like last night's footsteps and that gave me an idea.

Thump. Thump. Thump.

With everyone out and Armuth busy in the kitchen, I could go upstairs.

Thump. Thump. Thump.

I wasn't going to let that boy frighten me. Who did he think he was?

Thump. Thump. Thump.

I was going to find out.

Chapter Sixteen

With one eye on the kitchen I ran up the first flight of stairs. The shutters were open on the first floor and I could see the falling-apart barn and, a little behind it, old brown trees that went on for miles.

I raced up to the second floor, then the third, shaking my arms and puffing my chest like I'd seen Kitty do to get herself ready for a race. The boy couldn't tell me what to do. I threw my shoulders back. And I wasn't leaving till I knew exactly who he was and what he was doing up here.

When I opened the door, the mirror lay against the wall. My reflection spilled across its silver and grime mould. Suddenly I couldn't move. Now that I was here, his threat felt real, but at the same time I knew I couldn't stand another night listening to empty footsteps that seemed to follow me whatever room I was in. I was going to tell him to stop. He wasn't going freak me out any more.

I shook myself and forced my feet forward until I was standing in front of it. But the only thing the mirror showed was me in Fliss's clothes. I closed my eyes so I wouldn't have to look at all the pink and pressed my hands against it.

Nothing.

I opened my eyes, pressed harder.

Nothing.

Then, remembering the last time I was here, when the mirror had been pushed aside, I grabbed the edge, and with a slow, reluctant groan that was almost human, the mirror shifted aside. I pushed again so there'd be enough space for me to slip into the boy's room, but, once I'd moved the mirror, there was no doorway. There was only a wall.

I gulped, pressing my hands against it, feeling the lumps in the faded green-grey wallpaper. There'd been a door right here, I'd seen it; I'd been *through* it.

I ran my hands over the wallpaper.

A whole room, right here.

I picked at a piece of wallpaper and peeled a long strip off in a large curve, and that's when I heard the scuffling noise. It sounded muffled. I pressed my ear against the wall and listened. After a few minutes the scuffling began to sound a little like coughing. I stood back then knocked hard twice. The muffled noise stopped.

He was there! Now I just had to get in.

I felt around until I found a door shape in the wall. It slipped so seamlessly into the wallpaper that I had to keep my eyes trained on the outline, or it would disappear again. There wasn't a handle, but I found a small notch halfway down the right-hand side. I pressed it, felt a click, then the door slowly creaked inwards.

This time the room looked very different. The only light came from a sliver of sun creeping through the broken boards across the window and a lone lit candle sitting on the bedside table. The other candles sat around the room like little waxy statues. I looked from the tiny helpless flame to Julien. He really did look ill. His face was pale and his blond hair was plastered to his head, his nightshirt darkened with patches of sweat.

He was staring at me, his brow furrowed. He coughed, then croaked, 'You shouldn't be here. I told you.'

I held my ground.

'You'll catch it!' he said, pointing at me. 'Everyone does.'

'Catch what?'

His voice faltered and he dropped his arm. 'Please.'

And I realised then that he wasn't trying to be mean; he was scared.

'I'm fine!' I said, walking into the room. 'See?' I gave a sort of a half twirl, half shrug. 'I've seen you twice now, three times really, and I'm fine.'

He let his head fall back on his pillow. 'No one comes here.' His voice shook as he turned to me. 'The door was locked. I checked it. How did you get in?'

I marched to the bottom of his bed and rested my hands on the rails. 'I unlocked it.'

'You should leave,' he said. 'It's not safe. I'm not safe.'

I wondered how long he'd been here on his own. 'Well, it's too late then, isn't it?' I said. 'Because I've probably already got it, haven't I?'

Julien frowned. I grinned.

'You dress strangely,' he said, then grimaced as he tried to sit up.

I raised my eyebrows at what he was wearing, which looked a lot like a dress. Then I looked at all the pink I was wearing and shrugged. 'So do you,' I said.

He gestured to the bottom of his bed and I sat. It was the only place to sit. The bed and table were the only furniture in the room. He propped himself up, but straight away began coughing and hacking.

'What's wrong with you, anyway?'

Julien shrugged his shoulders and swallowed hard. 'I'm sick. I must be kept away from everyone.' He looked away, sneezed, and stared at the slice of sun through the boarded window. 'The sickness came to my home.'

I shivered. The little bit of sun only reached halfway across the room, but it wasn't that. There was something so serious in his voice that made me think perhaps I'd been a bit stupid. My hand drifted to my forehead, but it was cool. I shook myself. I was fine. I wasn't really sick. I'd made up the sneezing and coughing to get out of going with my aunt and uncle and I'd only popped in and out of his room.

'Do you want to go?' he said.

I heard the longing in his voice and shook my head. 'I'm fine,' I said.

I had so many questions I wanted to ask him: why he was here, why he was on his own and why he only wandered about at night, but there was something about the way he seemed so sad that stopped me. In the end, I asked the simplest one.

'Julien, tell me what happened. What about the sickness?'

He took a deep breath.

Chapter Seventeen

'A sickness came to our village and then to our home,' he said. 'My parents kept us safe, at first.' He coughed. 'There were many deaths. We thought we were safe, but the sickness travelled, and it found us.'

Sunlight moved across the walls and the candle burnt to a grey stub as Julien told me how his parents made arrangements to travel to his uncle's house. His mother was already sick by then.

'She started sneezing and coughing. Then she fell into a deep sleep and we couldn't wake her.' His hands shook as he poured himself a glass of water. 'By the time we were ready to leave, I was sick too.' He sipped and swallowed, wincing. 'I tried to hide it from my mother and stepfather. I don't know if they knew. I don't remember much.' He took another sip of water. 'The horses were wild and ran so fast I thought the carriage would tip over. It was cold – so cold my hands froze.'

He held out his hands and I winced. Red weals streaked his palms, as if something had stuck to them then been ripped off.

'There was shouting. I think it was the driver shouting at the horse. He did not want to take us. We had to pay a lot of money.'

He looked at me, then at his quilt. It was a sort of dirty yellow colour with a double purple border round the edge. Embroidered flowers in hundreds of different shades of brown entwined tiny green stalks and bloomed across the whole bed.

'My mother was on the floor of the carriage. She was hot and she had the rash.' Julien's fingers reached for his neck. He didn't speak for a moment.

'The rash?' I prompted.

He nodded. 'It crept so fast we could watch it crawl.'

His fingers traced up his neck and along his jaw. He was looking at me but his eyes were somewhere else.

'My stepfather was crying. I had never seen him cry. And his nose bled, but he did not seem to notice. He stroked my mother's hair, kept it off her face as her skin got hotter and hotter.' Julien looked at me. 'She was still beautiful.'

I nodded. I believed him.

'He tried to get her to sit up. They'd told us something about that, about the lungs.'

Julien's hands clutched his sheets.

'He shouted then. At her and at me, but the carriage jolted. We were going too fast and my head hit the side. I saw stars and was sick.' He closed his eyes. 'It was rotten in there, in the carriage. The air was foul. I heard him say a prayer for my mother. I heard him tell her to hold on, hold on, *mon ange*.' He paused. 'Then nothing.'

He looked down at his hands, as if embarrassed, then up at me. His eyes were so full of pain I could feel the sting.

'I have not seen either of them since.'

We sat in silence for a while, then Julien coughed, clutching his chest.

'And you don't remember anything else?' I said.

He shook his head, took a sip of water. 'When I woke up, I was here.' He gestured to the tiny attic room. 'I do not know where I am.'

'How long have you been here?' I said.

He shrugged.

A thousand thoughts ran through my head. First of all he'd said carriage, which was a bit weird, but more than that I kept thinking he must have been kidnapped. Except Armuth and Herman weren't the kidnapping kind. Well, Herman didn't seem to be; I wasn't quite sure about Armuth yet.

'Who looks after you?' I asked. 'Who brings you the water and stuff?'

A shadow crossed his face and he shuddered. 'There is a man, a servant. He comes only in the dark, at night. He leaves a tray with food and a jug of water. He wears a mask . . . an evil mask – a devil's mask – and he never looks at me.' He grabbed my hand. 'He won't tell me where my parents are! He won't tell me anything!'

I thought of the footsteps I heard at night. Ice dripped down my back.

Julien looked over his shoulder and I followed his gaze to a thick curtain.

'He comes from there,' he said, pointing.

My skin prickled all over, and I felt cold and hot at the same time, but I got off the bed to look. The curtain was velvet. It must have been a deep green once, but was faded and threadbare now, splattered with fuzzy worn patches and holes. The hem was tattered from where it had been swept aside and caught under the door.

'Behind,' Julien croaked.

I pulled the curtain back and felt it snag on the rough floorboards as I stared at the door behind it. I'd just reached out to grab the handle when Julien shouted.

'Don't!'

I let the curtain drop and it flew back into place.

His eyes were wide, his nostrils flared, but before he could say anything else I swept the curtain aside and tried the handle.

Nothing.

'It looks like the door's bolted, probably from the other side,' I said. Then I asked what had been worrying me. 'Julien? The man. Is he really tall?' I leant against the door. 'And old? With grey hair?'

When Julien shook his head I shut my eyes with relief. 'He is tall, but he is not old. His hair is black, I think.'

I breathed a quiet sigh. It wasn't Herman and it wasn't my uncle. But someone was keeping him here. Who were they? And did Armuth and Herman know what was going on? I opened my eyes. Julien was looking down at his hands. I didn't want to ask the next question, but I had to.

'Um, does he . . . ? I mean, are you all right? I mean, I know you're sick, but you're not hurt or anything?'

He didn't answer, but his shoulders were rigid. I sat back on the bed, a little closer than before.

'He leaves the tray inside the door. I have to leave the empty tray there. If I don't, I don't get any the next day.'

'Why?' I asked.

Julien shook his head. 'All I know is that no one can know I am here. He only spoke once. It feels like a long time ago. He said I must be silent, that no one but him would visit me and if anyone else ever came I should not shout or speak a word. If I told anyone who I was, it would mean the end.'

He looked at his hands and I went cold. He'd told me who he was. No wonder he was so freaked out when I found him; no wonder he'd tried to frighten me off.

'He said no one could know about me or the whole house would be in danger. It would mean the end of everything.'

Chapter Eighteen

I felt sick.

I'd never meant to put him in danger. At first, I'd only wanted to know if he was real, so I could prove to everyone I wasn't lying. Then I'd wanted to tell him to stop scaring me half to death by following me around at night. But now I knew he never left the room, so it couldn't have been him making the footsteps.

I looked back at the velvet curtain, then at the doorway I'd come through. Something was nagging at me, picking at the edges of my brain. I was thinking about when I first arrived at the house, but there was something I wasn't seeing. I tried to remember what it looked like from the outside as I walked back to the curtain.

'Leave it,' he said. 'There is nothing you can do.'

But I realised that the door behind the curtain couldn't go anywhere. It was on an outside wall. Julien's window was the last one on the top floor, and Armuth and Herman's house was completely on its own in the middle of nowhere. We'd driven down a really long drive to get here. The nearest house was miles away in the village, so this man couldn't have come from anywhere. I shivered. Were the footsteps his? Was he the ghost?

I whirled round so fast that Julien slopped water down himself. He was mopping it up as I inched closer. Then I leant in and pinched him hard on his arm.

'Ow!' He frowned and clutched his glass.

'Well,' I said, 'you're definitely not a ghost.'

'Of course I am not,' he said, rubbing his arm, then he looked up at me and started to laugh. I laughed too, but his turned into another coughing fit that wouldn't stop. Eventually he managed to take a breath. 'At least not yet, anyway.'

I bit my lip.

I looked back out of my door. If Julien wasn't a ghost, then his being shut up in here was really serious. I couldn't help thinking that, from what he'd said about the sickness, maybe it was more than a bad cold.

'Julien, do you know what the sickness is?' I asked.

He shook his head.

I tapped my foot on the floorboards.

If Armuth and Herman didn't know he was ill and being kept up here, then they should – and so should my aunt and uncle. Aunt Cece would never believe me and maybe Armuth wouldn't either, but Herman might.

'Julien, I'm going to go and get help.'

But he wasn't listening. 'We had so many plans for the summer,' he said.

I looked at the sliver of sun peeking through the boards across the window. 'It's still summer,' I said, shrugging. 'I'm on my holidays.'

He leant forward. 'We were due to travel to my father's house in time for my fourteenth birthday, August twenty-eighth. When the sickness came, my parents decided we would leave much sooner. My uncle would understand, they said, and the summer would give me time to learn about the land.' He took a breath. 'I am due to inherit my father's home and lands when I reach fourteen.' He coughed, wiping away spittle with the back of his hand. 'They've been kept in trust by my uncle. He disapproved of my mother remarrying – and to an Englishman.'

'That's how you know such good English?' I said.

He smiled. 'Thank you, yes. We spent most of my childhood in England; I liked it very much. And my stepfather, I like him too.' His voice softened. 'I love him. He makes my mother happy and he is the only father I have ever known. My father died when I was young. I don't remember him.'

He paused for a moment, then his eyes lit up. 'I have so many ideas from my stepfather: how to make the land work for the estate and for the people, but also to make them beautiful. My stepfather studied botany for many years. He has such exciting ideas for the gardens. We would sit and discuss them.' He grinned. 'He lent me some of his books.'

He picked one from a small pile on the floor next to his bed. It had a brown cover with gold swirls, dots and leaf shapes across it.

'Here.'

He opened it and I stared. There were beautiful drawings of plants and vegetables and flowers, but that wasn't all. It was in mint condition. It smelt sweet, like vanilla and almonds. I turned to the front page. It said *la première impression, 1898. Première impression?* Didn't that mean first edition? This was seriously old.

Julien began to cough, clutching his chest. '1898 is supposed to be a great year, for me, for the estate, for all of us, but now I am stuck here and have the sickness and will die. I will never get to the house and all the plans will come to nothing.' He slumped back into his pillow.

I stared at him. Julien wiped damp hair back off his forehead. He wasn't joking.

'What did you just say?' I asked, his words ringing in my ears.

He didn't seem to notice how carefully I asked the question and nodded.

'I hoped it was summer,' he said. 'I hoped to get a message to my uncle that I was alive, but I don't know how long I've been here. It could be days, weeks, perhaps months. I sleep a lot. I think the servant gives me something to make me sleep, something in the food, so I don't know the day exactly. I only know day from night by the light through the window. It was cold, now the sun is hotter, so I know some time has passed.'

I cocked my head to the side. '1898 is supposed to be a great year?' I said slowly.

'Yes,' he said and smiled sadly. 'But I am sick now and . . .'

He carried on talking, but I tuned him out, watching him closely for a sign he was teasing me. I thought about prodding him again to check he wasn't a ghost.

'August twenty-eighth is the day I am to sign,' he said. Sadness crossed his face like a grey cloud and he closed his eyes. His voice fell to a whisper. 'I would have come of age and inherited my father's estate, Maison de Noyer.'

I gasped. 'Maison de Noyer? That's this house!'

Julien's eyes snapped open. His brows furrowed.

'It's true. I'm staying in Maison de Noyer. I saw the sign as we drove in. It was hanging off the gate.'

'It is not possible.' Julien looked around him.

'It's true,' I said.

'But that would mean . . .' He looked straight at me and we both spoke at the same time. 'My uncle!'

'Your uncle!'

'It's him. The man in the mask. It's him keeping me here.'

I looked down at my hands. Julien didn't seem to be lying, but I couldn't see how he could be telling the truth either. I mean, where was his uncle now and where did that door lead? And what did he mean about it being 1898?

'Julien,' I said carefully, watching him take ragged breaths, 'why would your uncle keep you prisoner?' I shrugged. 'Unless . . .'

'Unless he planned to try to claim the estate for himself,' Julien finished. His face was flushed.

'But what about your mother?' I asked.

Julien wrinkled his nose. 'A woman cannot inherit!' he said, as if that was obvious. 'And she married an Englishman.' He threw off his covers and tried to swing his legs round. 'The house and lands were entrusted to my uncle until my birthday, but . . .'

'But what about the whole 1898 thing?' I asked, waiting for him to laugh at me because this had to be his fever talking. I began to wonder just how much of anything he said was actually true. It was a good story and I should know, I'd made plenty up, but I'd never gone this far.

'It was agreed I would sign by my birthday,' Julien said patiently. 'If there is no heir, the land becomes forfeit to my uncle as custodian.'

He looked at me. 'And there is no heir if I am hidden up here or . . .' He gulped.

'Dead.'

He held his head in his hands. 'It is over. The man was right. The end of everything.'

'No!'

Julien didn't respond.

'You have to get better, Julien. You must! And I can help you. Except there's something . . . well, something I have to tell you.' I was fidgeting, picking at my nails and trying to find a way to say it without freaking him out. He looked pale enough as it was.

'Tell me,' he said, looking up and grabbing my arm where my scar was. His hand was warm. I could feel its heat through my cardigan.

'Julien,' I began, and swallowed. My throat was tight, but I needed to say something. He needed to know, even if he was sick.

'Julien, today is August twenty-sixth.' I took another breath. 'But there's something else.' I took a deep breath. 'It's not 1898 any more.'

Chapter Nineteen

'Julien?'

He stared past me at the room beyond the mirror, frowning at something I couldn't see and clutching his glass of water so tightly I worried it might break.

'Did you hear me?'

He didn't answer. He hadn't said a word since I'd told him what the year was.

'It's true. You can come with me and see for yourself,' I said. 'Right now.'

'What about your family?'

'It's fine,' I said, my eyes sliding away from his. 'My parents won't mind at all.'

He shook his head.

I followed his gaze. The room beyond the mirror still seemed to shimmer. I wondered if he saw that too.

Suddenly he turned to me. 'Where did you come

from really? It is cruel to lie.'

I looked at the floor, then back at him. 'I'm not lying, Julien, I promise. I came from your house.'

The dinner bell clanged, shattering the silence. My stomach gurgled.

'I can prove it,' I said. 'Come with me, now.'

He looked into my eyes. I saw something there. A glimmer from the candlelight behind him, but maybe a little curiosity too.

'We'll go through together,' I said, holding out my hand.

There was a pause, then he smiled. He put down his glass of water and took my hand. It felt clammy, but sure.

'Right,' I said, pulling us forward.

'Wait.'

I stopped.

Julien looked at me. 'The future is through there? This is what you're telling me.'

I bit my lip.

'And your parents . . . they will wear clothes like yours?'

I looked down at Fliss's top and leggings, then back at Julien in his old nightshirt. I shook my head.

'I make most of my clothes, but not this outfit. This was given to me.'

'You're a seamstress?'

I laughed. 'No. I just like making things. You know, like a hobby?'

He raised his eyebrows. 'Yes! I like reading books and chess. I could teach you.'

I nodded. 'Okay.'

He grinned.

I looked over at the room on my side of the mirror, then back at Julien's hand, still in mine.

'And they will help me?'

'Who?'

'Your parents?'

I stopped breathing for a second then something rushed out before I could think.

'Absolutely. They're brilliant. They'll help you get better, they'll get you clothes and they'll look after you. They're amazing. They can do anything.'

Julien smiled.

I felt a gnawing in the pit of my stomach for lying, but it was too late to take it back. The words had just tumbled out like always. I only wanted him to come with me and be okay.

The dinner bell shrilled and we both jumped.

'Come on.' I pulled him towards the mirror. 'Everything's going to be all right.'

I stepped through the doorway, but my right arm

jerked backwards, as if Julien had pulled it hard.

I turned and saw him standing in the doorway. 'Come on,' I said.

He shook his head.

'I promise, everything will be great.'

Julien reached his hand out to mine, then dropped it.

I reached my hand through to his, but he shook his head.

'I cannot go.' He began to cough.

'Look it's all right,' I said. 'I'll go and get help.'

He doubled over, clutching his sides.

The dinner bell shrilled again. Longer this time.

'I'll come back, I promise.'

Julien stepped away, looking at me as if I wasn't really there.

'Trust me,' I said.

'I am sick and you're not real,' he said, shaking his head. 'It's not true, what you say.'

'I'll prove it,' I said. I looked around his room and saw a small pile of books under his bed. 'One of your books. Give me the one that's brand new.'

He picked up the brown and gold book and turned towards me.

The bell shrilled.

'Look, I have to go,' I said, 'but I won't be long.' I

held my hand out for the book.

'Maybe there's another copy of this in the library,' I said. 'Or maybe they'll be able to date it for me and I can prove to you where I'm from.'

'Your parents?'

I bit my top lip and nodded.

Julien turned to face me, his eyes strangely blank and fixed on mine. The air between us shimmered.

'You will come back?'

I nodded, reached in and took the book from his hand. I was about to say something when his door slammed shut between us. I jumped away as the mirror slid across into place.

'Julien?'

I lifted a hand to knock but saw something in the mirror. The book in my hand had opened to a page filled with flowers. Something about it itched in my brain, then I remembered. The books by my bed! The one I'd touched had pictures just like this, only covered in mould. I felt a shiver. I turned to the first page of the book and stared at the date. 1898. Then I ran down the stairs, skidded along the corridor, and flung the door of my room open.

There were only two books sitting on the bedside table now, not three.

I shut my eyes and opened them again, but the

mouldy old book I'd stuffed under the others was gone. Well, not exactly gone. I clasped the brand new book, the gold swirls on its cover shining, its pages mould-free and smelling of fresh vanilla. It wasn't in the stack because it was here in my hand. I gulped. It really was from 1898. So did that mean Julien was too?

Chapter Twenty

I heard Armuth calling and stuffed the book underneath the others, exactly like before. Then I ran to dinner.

It was just three of us. Armuth explained that my aunt, uncle and cousins had decided to stay with their relatives for another day – something about the weather being bad or the old lady being ill, I wasn't sure as I wasn't really listening. I was still thinking about Julien, at least, until Armuth's next question.

'Do you want to telephone?'

I raised an eyebrow.

'To speak to Cece?' she said.

I shook my head and made a face.

'She would like to speak to you, I am sure. I think she must care for you very much,' Armuth said.

I looked up and gave a little laugh.

'Not really. I haven't seen her in a while. Well,

six months,' I said, pulling at a loose thread on Fliss's cardigan. Then I remembered what my aunt had said about not talking too much to Armuth and I went quiet.

Armuth frowned as she set out a plate of cold, sliced chicken and a potato salad with bits in, which I picked out till Herman raised both bushy eyebrows. He must have eaten already because he didn't have a plate. The bits turned out to be chives and were nice and oniony. I was starving and helped myself to seconds and thirds.

No one spoke, which meant I could concentrate on ways to help Julien, but I couldn't see how. I couldn't bring him into my side of the house, not if he wouldn't come. I thought of what I'd said to him about my parents being here on holiday and them being totally fine about him, and my cheeks burnt. Then I thought about the book I'd just hidden in my room and shivered. It really was straight out of 1898, but did that mean he was too? Couldn't it be a trick? But then I remembered him coughing. He'd said he was sick and he looked sick. Whatever the truth was, he needed a doctor. I thought about asking Aunt Cece for help, but pictured her completely freaking out and shook my head. I needed to make a proper plan. I'd have to ask Armuth and Herman.

I toyed with my fork for ages, then looked up.

'Um,' I said, 'I found a boy's clothes in the wardrobe in my room. Who's are they?'

Armuth had been reaching for the salad and froze. A thick tension filled the kitchen.

She started to say something, then bit her lip. She turned to Herman and I saw a tear slide down her cheek, closely followed by another and another. She reached for my arm, gave it a gentle squeeze, but before I realised what was happening she'd left the table, leaving her plate half eaten. I looked at Herman.

'What did I say? I didn't mean to upset her. I'm sorry. I'm really sorry.'

He didn't answer, simply nodded for me to finish eating, but I wasn't hungry any more. I busied myself clearing the table and sneaking a few looks at Herman until I was sure he wasn't angry with me.

'It's just that they're old – really old – the boy's clothes,' I said to him. 'I know they look like dresses, but I think maybe a boy would wear them. You know, like a nightshirt?'

Herman stared. I held still and forced myself not to look away, even though it felt as if he could see straight into my head. He didn't say a word. Instead he walked out of the kitchen.

'It was only a question,' I said to the empty room.

I washed up the dishes and stacked the plates, all the while thinking about Julien's illness. He was definitely sick. His chest was obviously bad and he didn't look well.

They must have had all sorts of illnesses years ago that you didn't get now. But the whole 1898 thing was weird.

I hung the wet cloth over the tap. I had to tell someone. If I was going to get him better, I'd need help. Julien would probably hate me, but maybe I could try again with Herman – at least he'd listen.

Just as I was thinking of him, he walked back into the kitchen.

'Herman?'

Herman shook his head and gestured to the old blue dresser where the papers had been. The papers! My heart started beating fast.

The dresser had once been a pretty sky blue, but was peeling so much now I could see through to the wood underneath. A thick coil of paint curled on top and I resisted the urge to pull it off. I opened the two latticed doors. The bottom shelf was stuffed full of old kitchen equipment, but the top shelf held only a square, smooth wooden box. I looked back at Herman and felt a spark of excitement when he nodded his permission. I lifted the box out and placed it lightly on the kitchen table. Every edge of the box was round and smooth. I traced the swirling grain of the wood with my fingers. Where a tiny key would fit in the top was inlaid with mother-of-pearl. But I was more excited about what was inside.

'Can I open it?' I said and he nodded, pointing at me then back at the box. 'It's for me?'

Herman nodded.

I could feel a smile work its way round the edges of my mouth as I lifted the top of the box. Then it fell. The papers weren't there. Then I realised what it was. 'It's a sewing box.'

Herman nodded. I looked inside.

It was beautiful. The lid was lined in a soft baby blue padded satin and darted across in a diamond pattern. The top shelf was a maze of tiny, perfect compartments filled with threads, needles, buttons and pins. It had a lip on one side and pulling gently on it, the whole section lifted up. Underneath, lined in the same blue, were reels and reels of cotton, ribbons and small packets of different coloured beads.

'Er, Herman? Is this for me to borrow?'

But Herman did his pointing thing between me and the box again and I realised he was giving it to me.

I flashed him a grin.

'I mean, wow,' I said, slotting the top tray back in place, the lid shutting with a pleasing click. 'Thanks, Herman, it's amazing. I can make some brilliant stuff with this.'

I stared at my pink leggings and the T-shirt that looked as if a punnet of strawberries had been thrown at it, then towards my room where the old clothes hung in the wardrobe. When I glanced towards him, Herman was nodding.

'You mean I can use the old clothes?' I asked. 'The ones in my room? Are you sure?'

When he nodded again I struggled to find any words for such a totally brilliant gift. All I could come up with was, 'But they're *really* old – like proper *vintage* old and, well, amazing!'

He shrugged. I grinned from ear to ear.

Herman left the kitchen before I could hug him, and back in my room I found the light had been fixed. I touched the edge of the nightshirt that looked like Julien's, then let it go. I chose two smocks from the wardrobe instead and spread them out on the bed. One was full of moth holes, but the lacy collar was just about perfect. I shook out the cricks in my shoulders.

I looked up at the ceiling as if I could see through to Julien's attic. I'd figure out a plan to help him while I worked. It would only take a few minutes and I hadn't made anything for ages. I sat on the cot, opened the sewing box and reached for a needle and thread.

But I spent longer than I meant to. I let my guard down and I shouldn't have, because the next thing I knew, someone was screaming my name.

Chapter Twenty-One

'Angela? Angela! Wake up!'

Black smoke hung heavy and thick in my bedroom. The minute I took a breath it choked me.

A misshapen monster reared from my bedroom door. I tried to scream, but the smoke snatched away the sound, leaving me coughing until I was hollowed out. The monster turned to face me.

'Help!' I croaked.

But the monster shuffled closer. I huddled deeper into my bed and clung on to the headboard.

'No!'

But as it reached the foot of my bed the monster flung off its skin and it was my dad inside. I reached out to him, my eyes smarting, my bones shaking as panic crept beneath my skin and rattled them.

'Daddy!' My voice crackled. I hadn't called him that in

forever. 'What's happening?'

But he didn't answer and I choked on my words. He turned to the window and ripped the curtains aside. Mum would be really angry, I thought, as one half fell off the rail and disappeared into the black. A flashing blue light filled the room.

'Daddy?'

He threw the duvet he'd been hiding under over me. I screamed, but my throat was like sandpaper and nothing came out.

'Daddy,' I whispered into the fabric.

I heard breaking glass and shouting voices.

'Daddy, what's happening?'

He swept me up in his arms and the duvet slid to the ground. I reached for it, but he pulled me away.

'Daddy?'

The blue light flickered on, off, on, off. A freezing draught trailed goosebumps up the back of my arms. The rest of me was so hot it hurt. I was swung round fast and found myself staring at a man with a bushy beard that threatened to take over his face. As my dad pushed me through my bedroom window into the bushy man's arms, I screamed. I looked to my right and saw jagged glass. I pulled my arm back, but wriggling only made the cut deeper. I screamed again and the man tightened his grip, pulling me through.

'Sir, please!' he shouted at the window behind me, but it was empty now. My dad wasn't there any more. He'd disappeared into the smoke, which wasn't black any more; it was red, yellow and orange.

'Fire!' I croaked.

The man shifted me to one strong arm and began to climb down his ladder, away from my window.

'No! Daddy!'

I struggled to reach back, but it was useless; the man's arm was like iron and my punches and kicks made no difference. He reached the bottom and put me on the wet grass. I watched him run to a huge fire engine parked in our driveway. All around me the blue lights flashed. The sky was dark. My house glowed like it was alive.

Neighbours spilt out of their houses. People stood on the streets in their dressing gowns and slippers as firemen rushed and shouted to each other. But something was missing. My heartbeat slowed to a stop. I stared up at my window, but I couldn't see it for flames.

Suddenly my heart began to pound, beating in my ribcage and throat, and filling my head with its thump.

'Daddy!' I screamed. 'Mum! Dad! Ben!'

The flames licked closer and closer. Their heat washed over me. There was a roar and a whine and a sound like sticks breaking. I took a step towards my house, then another and another. The heat doubled, then tripled. It was hot, so hot.

'Daddy!'

I bolted upright.

The hot morning sun shone straight through the gap between the shutters onto my face. Bits of lace and threads covered the bedspread. I tried to brush them off but my hands shook. They were sticky with sweat. I swallowed, sat up, and took deep shuddering breaths. My insides felt like jelly.

I ran to the bathroom to wash the taste of ash from my mouth and the sweat stuck to my skin. The nightmare picked at me, but I forced my feet back to my room, pretending it wasn't there.

The smock I'd worked on last night lay on the bed. It had been really frayed with a massive hole at the front but now looked like a floaty blouse with a lace collar. It looked almost perfect with Fliss's pink leggings and I allowed myself a few seconds in front of the mirror to admire my stitching. It was a little loose under one arm and down the hem on the left side, but I could fix that later. It looked old, but modern at the same time. It looked like –

'Julien!'

I felt sick. It had been forever since I'd done any

sewing, but that was no excuse, I'd forgotten all about him and the nightmare was my punishment.

I felt my face flush as I raced to the stairs, but Herman waved me into the kitchen. Inside I found pots of jams on the table with names I didn't recognise and Armuth pulling a tray of hot croissants out of the oven.

'Take as many as you like,' she said.

Remembering how hungry I'd been the day before, I took three.

'They will not be back until late, I think,' Armuth said.

'Perfect,' I said.

'Then tomorrow, of course, you will all be leaving.'

I could feel her studying me as I nibbled the edge of a pastry.

'Well, perhaps some fresh air will be good for you today.'

I slumped against the door, a huge flake of pastry on my chin.

'No more stuck inside, yes?'

'It's okay,' I said, nodding like crazy, 'I like being inside. Please?'

Armuth gave me a small smile. 'But your aunt. You understand, she insists.'

I nodded reluctantly and spun on my heels, the blouse flaring out behind me.

'Wait?'

She was looking at me strangely now. Then I realised she was staring at my new top. Her mouth twitched, she sucked her cheeks in and brought a hand to her heart.

'It was Herman,' I said quickly. 'He said it was okay. He said –'

'Herman?' she said, shaking her head, her eyebrows knitted together. Then she brought a hand to her mouth and squeezed her eyes tightly, but it didn't stop the sob escaping. 'Angela, I must tell you . . .' She leant in, then seemed to change her mind and turned away.

'Wait, Armuth?' I said, but she didn't wait. She ran towards the annexe and the swing door slammed and slammed and slammed behind her.

Chapter Twenty-Two

My croissant turned to paper in my mouth. I put the others back on the table.

Herman poked his head round, nodded solemnly for me to go, then left himself. I kicked the edge of my chair. This was so unfair. Armuth was upset, but I hadn't done anything wrong.

The door to the annexe opened again, scraping along the floor, so I scooted out of the kitchen. I eventually tracked down my trainers, but struggled to get them on. Aunt Cece had shrunk them, their tongues hanging out like dogs panting for water. I nudged a pair I thought might be hers until they were completely hidden beneath a pile of muddy wellington boots and felt a little better.

Outside the sky was as bright blue as a kid's painting. The sun warmed my head as I turned to look up at the house. I counted the windows along the top floor.

One, two, three, four, five, six, seven, eight.

I shook my head, squeezed my eyes shut and remembered trying all the handles of the doors on the third floor.

I opened my eyes again, but there were no extra windows, no extra room. There was nowhere for the servant to come from the other side of Julien's room.

I shivered even though it was hot. I turned back towards the house, but Armuth was standing in the doorway watching me, her arms limp by her side, her shoulders slumped. It was odd, though. She was looking at me as if she was trying to find an answer to something. I felt so bad about upsetting her, even though I didn't understand how. I gave a small, sorry smile and made a wide circle in the gravel as if I'd planned to do that all along, as if I hadn't been thinking about going back inside and up the stairs.

I gave the barn a wide berth too, even though Kitty and Fliss were miles away, and walked around to the orchard I'd seen from the first floor the other day. It was much bigger up close.

The trees were tall, though each was brown and bare. The grass was a stiff yellow straw and the deeper I went in, the darker and cooler it got. My feet kept finding little hard stones. I pocketed one then kicked another and another. Then my foot hit something harder.

'Owwww.'

A large stone thumped heavily onto its back.

'Oops.'

I kneeled, parting the grass around it. Dew soaked my leggings and seeped into my trainers. The stone was a rounded lump with something carved onto the bit that peeked out of the ground. I pulled more grass away from the base, making my sleeves soggy.

I shivered.

I'd found a grave.

There was another lump of stone just behind this one, then another behind that, and another and another. I sat on my heels. This wasn't an orchard; it was a graveyard.

I pushed the headstone back up, then stood and tiptoed around it. The sun began to break through the trees as the graves grew further apart. They were worn, shrunken and so old I couldn't read most of the inscriptions.

My breath was coming loud and fast. My hands clutched the hem of my smock, damp now from the wet grass. I turned to go back when something caught my eye. It was a grave sticking up a little further than the others. A grave with an inscription I could make out, a name I recognised. The grave was for someone named Julien.

Forgetting everything, I used my sleeves to clear the dirt from the rest of the stone.

As I pulled away shreds of clinging moss and clods of mud, the grave revealed the full name of Julien Nicolas Bastien, followed by two dates. One of them was 1898, but it was the second date. The first was 1884. I quickly did the maths in my head. This Julien was fourteen.

I traced my fingers over the numbers. The date for Julien Nicolas Bastien's death was August 28, 1898.

I felt sick.

Then I shook myself because it wasn't possible. There was no way it could be the same Julien. But the grave was solid beneath my hands and the dates added up.

I knelt in the wet grass and ticked over the facts.

I'd spoken to Julien and I'd touched him, so he couldn't be a ghost.

Fact.

He thought it was 1898.

Fact.

But that was well over a hundred years ago.

Fact.

As the sun dappled through the trees and touched the top of the grave, I closed my eyes.

If Julien was sick enough to think it was 1898, then he needed my help. If he somehow really was in 1898, then he still needed my help. Because in two days he would die. He didn't have anyone else and neither did I. Maybe that was why it was me who found him. Maybe I was meant to help him, to make up for what I did.

My nightmare slithered into my head. I felt ash in my mouth, heard the crackle and spit of flames and shoved it all back down as far as I could.

Goosebumps prickled up my spine. I shut my eyes tight.

'Daddy!'

Blue lights flashed across my eyes; I saw a bushy beard then felt the sting of broken glass on the inside of my right arm. I shook myself.

I couldn't help them, but I could try to warn Julien. This was my chance to make things right.

I started to run towards the house.

'Julien,' I shouted. 'I'm coming.'

Chapter Twenty-Three

I raced into the house and straight up the stairs. Nothing was going to stop me getting to Julien now. Not even Armuth.

I made it to the first-floor landing, but stopped short when I heard the squeak of straining steps above me. I bolted back down the stairs, throwing myself behind the nearest tapestry just in time as she plodded down.

It was musty behind the hanging and the wall behind me was so cold it felt wet. I flattened myself against it, holding my breath as Armuth's squeaky shoes reached the bottom step. Then she stopped.

'Angela?'

I held still, my stomach pumping, my chest shaking. My lungs felt like they'd burst. Spots like stars flew across my eyes, but just when I thought I might explode, Armuth headed off to the kitchen. As soon as I heard the door shut, I took a gulp of breath, slipped out and rushed back upstairs.

When I reached the third floor I barrelled down the corridor and flung open the door. The mirror lay flat against the wall, covering the connecting door. I gripped the edge of the mirror and began to push, but it wouldn't budge. I tried again, but it wouldn't move. I took a deep breath, then pushed and pushed and pushed, but the mirror stayed still.

I looked into it and saw myself, red-faced and covered in grass stains and dirt, but nothing else. There were no ripples, nothing at all. It looked like any old normal mirror. I felt a sudden stab of fear in my stomach. I could hear Aunt Cece's voice in my head saying, 'Stop telling stories.' I could see the windows from outside, eight all together and no extra room on the end, but Julien was in there, I knew it.

'Come on,' I said. 'Open!'

My hands were pink and pocked where the bevelled edge of the mirror had dug into my skin. It reminded me of the welts across Julien's palms and I pushed with everything I had. My hands smarted so much it brought tears to my eyes, but I kept on pushing and, slowly, the mirror gave a straining groan as it shifted sideways.

The door behind was shut tight, flush to the wallpaper, but I knew where to look for the catch now, and when I opened the door, I felt giddy.

Julien was sat up in his bed. His mouth hung open for a second before he replaced it with a huge grin. Then he reached for something on the floor, managed to grab the end, but couldn't seem to lift it back up. I watched him struggle, still thinking about his grave outside then my brain caught up with what I was seeing. He was here and he was alive! It might be 1898, but we had time. I ran over and grabbed the box. It was a chessboard.

'You're back,' he said, panting with exertion, but smiling, 'and I am going to teach you to play.' He stopped suddenly, studying me. 'What's the matter?'

I was lost for words. It was amazing that he was here, but now I was over being relieved, I wasn't sure how to tell him that where I came from, he'd been dead for over a hundred years.

'Angela?'

I shook my head.

He frowned then reached for the board in my hands. 'Angela?'

'It's tomorrow!' I blurted.

He smiled. 'My birthday, yes.' He dropped his arms. 'But, Angela, you have made me think.' He pushed his fringe off his face. 'I am going to speak to the servant and get him to bring my uncle. I am going to tell him that I can sign and I can inherit the house. I am ready. No one has to see that I am sick, so long as they have my papers. I know how to make the land work. I can make all the plans from here, at least until I am well.'

My fingers clutched the box. I could smell the leather, feel how shiny and new it was.

'And I must be well, Angela. I must get better.' He sat up. 'I know that now. Because of what you said.' He smiled. '*You have to get better and everything will be all right,* that's what you said.' He nodded. 'Maybe I am already better, yes?'

But when I didn't answer, he raised his eyebrows. 'It is a good plan, no?'

I bit my bottom lip.

'Angela?'

'The thing is, Julien,' I said, then realising I was still holding the chessboard, I put it down on his bed. 'If this is your uncle's house, why hasn't he said anything? Why hasn't he come to see you?' I scuffed a foot against a loose floorboard. 'I mean, why has he kept you here like, well, like a prisoner?'

Julien frowned.

'You said you don't know how long you've been here, so why would he treat you like this?'

'I've been too sick,' Julien said, his nose in the air.

'But you're not too sick to sign some documents, surely?'

'Well, I have to be fourteen to sign,' he said, crossing his arms. 'It has to be on my birthday. Perhaps he's been planning it for tomorrow. Perhaps I have been worrying for nothing!'

'Perhaps your uncle isn't as nice as you think!' I shouted.

Julien flicked his fringe off his face but it fell straight back. I could tell I was making him angry, but I didn't care. There wasn't time. I couldn't just let him die tomorrow. I had to warn him, give him a chance.

'You don't know,' I said, 'and you can't trust him. He's had you locked up in here since forever.'

'Keeping me safe!' he yelled. 'People died of this sickness. Our whole village – probably my mother.'

As he realised what he'd said, Julien's face began to crumple. He clenched his jaw and squeezed his eyes shut, but when that didn't work he looked away, letting his fringe flop over his eyes.

'My stepfather too,' he continued quietly. 'Otherwise they would have come for me, I know it.'

I reached out to touch his shoulder and he didn't shrug me off. When he spoke again he was calmer.

'It is only one more day then the whole house will be mine. I can sign the papers then fix the lands so they work. I remember everything my stepfather taught me – everything.' He gave me a small smile. 'I thought there was no hope, then you came. You listened to me, you understood how lonely I was and you became my friend. Now I just need to be well. Help me, Angela.'

Something warm bloomed in my chest. Then he looked at my hand on his shoulder as if he'd just noticed it, and up at me. I snatched my hand back and fiddled with the edge of my blouse. My cheeks felt hot. I could still feel him looking at me.

'It is so good you are back, Angela. I was alone for a long time. I thought, perhaps you were a . . .' He smiled. 'But you are here. And you are wrong about this. I must get my uncle to see me.'

I shook my head. I couldn't dislodge the image of the gravestone and the two dates inscribed on it.

'I could show you the whole house. My mother told me the grounds are beautiful.' He closed his eyes and smiled. 'We have so many plans. I studied all of my stepfather's notes. Years ago, this house was famous for its walnut trees. My stepfather wrote two books on this subject. Did I tell you? He said I had a talent. I can make it happen. I can make the lands prosperous and the estate will thrive again.'

Something cold slid down my spine. The grave hadn't said what Julien died of, only that he'd died on August 28. I thought about the book sitting by my bedside table, the one that was actually from 1898. Then I thought about the servant in the mask, the man he called the devil, the same man he was hoping would bring his uncle. Did Julien die because he was sick or because of the servant or his uncle or –

'No!' I shouted.

'What do you mean, no?'

'I mean, what if your uncle's not a good man? What if he hasn't been keeping you here till your birthday? What if he's planning to keep you up here forever?'

Julien frowned. 'But, Angela,' he said slowly, 'how would you know?' Then his face changed. He looked at the room beyond the mirror then back at me. 'What do you know?'

I bit my lip. 'Nothing,' I said, sitting on his bed, crossing my legs and pulling my sleeves over my hands. 'But just say it goes wrong? What if he doesn't come and you're still stuck up here? What then? I'm supposed to go home tomorrow.'

'Back to England?'

I nodded. 'And it'll be too late for me to help you get better and you'll be on your own and –' I paused. Then in a small voice I asked, 'What if you never leave?'

I looked at my hands as I remembered Armuth's ghost story.

'You're sick, you said so, and I want to help you, but . . .' I gulped. 'You have to come with me. Now.'

I thought of the grave outside, of the first version of the book I saw, all crumbling and covered in mould. If he stayed he'd die.

'Julien,' I said, 'it's the only way.' I gulped. 'Trust me. It's your last chance.'

Chapter Twenty-Four

Julien's face went grey. His eyes darted around the room and settled on my doorway. He stared through into the other room. After a moment he said, 'I cannot leave.'

I looked at the open doorway, the gently shimmering air beyond. What would happen if Julien really did come with me? I opened my mouth to speak, but he spoke first.

'Not without my mother and stepfather.' He looked at me. 'I have to know for certain they are gone. That there's no chance they will come for me.' Then he looked at his hands. 'And there's danger to the house. The man said if anyone knew about me, it would be the end.' He coughed and his chest rattled.

'But what does that even mean?' I said. 'What danger to the house?'

Julien's brow furrowed and his eyes darted around the room as if he was looking for the answer. Then he looked up, caught my eyes and slowly shook his head.

'What?' I asked.

'We heard stories,' he said in a whisper, 'at home. But they were rumours, nothing but childish tales to frighten the villagers. Except . . .'

He paused and I wanted to shake him.

'What?' I said, my voice unnaturally high.

'They burn the houses,' he said, his eyes wide. 'If people are sick, they burn them and anything or anyone inside them.'

I gasped. His words felt like a punch to my chest, right between my ribs. I forgot to breathe. I forgot how to.

Julien nodded. 'They say it stops the sickness from spreading.'

Something snapped inside of me.

'Come with me, now,' I said, taking his hand.

'With your mother and father?' he said.

I turned away to look at the velvet curtain and squeezed his hand. 'Yeah. Look, the most important thing is to get you out of here.'

But my hands were shaking, and he noticed.

'What is wrong?' He stared at my hands. 'What has happened?'

I looked away.

'What do you know?' he asked again.

I turned to face him. My voice sounded like it was

coming from far away. Julien's face was inches from mine.

'You're about to die,' I whispered.

He took my hand and placed my palm against his chest. His skin felt paper thin and boiling hot. I could feel his heart fluttering like a small bird trying to escape a cage. I felt a creeping blush on my cheeks.

He leant in close. 'We both know I am going to die.'

Then he let go and started coughing again. My hand stayed on his chest. When he noticed, I snatched it, hiding it behind my back.

'No,' I said, shaking my head. 'No!'

I thought of the grave and Julien lying in it forever, and I knew I had to tell him it was going to happen sooner than he realised, but I couldn't find the words.

'What are you so afraid of?' he asked.

I shook my head.

'Tell me,' he said, taking my hand again and this time holding it to him. His heart beat into my hands. I looked into his eyes.

'Tell me,' he said.

I took a deep breath.

'I saw something.' I looked away. 'Outside, in the gardens. I saw your . . .' I let my hand drop. I couldn't say it.

'I never thought I would leave here,' he said quietly.

I was about to speak when an ear-splitting car horn

echoed through the doorway. Julien dropped my hand and stared behind me.

'What is that?'

I stood up. 'I have to go.'

'But that sound . . .'

'It's my mum and dad,' I said, to cover any more questions. The horn honked again and he flinched. I took a step towards him then forced myself towards the mirror. As I stepped through the doorway he called for me.

'*Ange?*'

But I was already turning back. 'I'll be back soon,' I said. 'I'm going to think of something. We have to make sure that you don't d–' I took a breath. 'We have to make sure you get your inheritance. You have to hold on till I get back, okay? Don't say anything to the servant. Promise?'

He nodded.

'You have to hold on, Julien. You have to!'

I stepped back as the mirror slid shut with such a loud *thunk* it shook the floorboards.

I heard car doors open and slam shut. I knew they'd be looking for me so I raced downstairs, but as I neared the first floor, I slowed to a stop, thinking.

The way the mirror shut . . . It was quicker this time, and it had been harder to push open – much harder than the time before and the time before that. It was getting harder to open each time I went up there. Would I even be able to open it again?

I gazed up, as if I could see through the stairs to the mirror, but a firm grip on my wrist latched onto me before I could do anything else.

Chapter Twenty-Five

'Get. Down. Now.'

The hand belonged to my aunt. Her mouth puckered as if it was full of sour chews.

'Where's Armuth?'

'I-I-I don't know.'

She lunged, pulling me down the stairs to the main hallway. When we reached the bottom she let go of my arm like she was throwing it away.

'I had permission to be up there,' I said, thrusting my shoulders back.

She narrowed her eyes, but before she could say anything Kitty, Fliss and my uncle walked in. My cousins were carrying bulging plastic bags in each hand, two in Fliss's case, but Kitty stared at the floor and Fliss's eyes were red.

'What's all this then, eh?' Uncle Vaughn said, hooking

his leg round the door to shut it.

No one spoke.

Aunt Cece rounded on him, gesturing at me. 'See? She's not even trying to behave.'

Uncle Vaughn sagged, as if she'd pushed all the air out of him. He put down his bags.

'Listen, love, I'm sure Angela's got an explanation for whatever it is she's supposed to have done.' He gave me a quick, tired smile and reached out to my aunt who twitched away.

'Oh, I am sure she will,' she said, waving a hand that made me duck.

She spun round to face me, lowered her voice till it was dangerously quiet, then smiled, showing all her teeth.

'If you've spoken to Armuth . . . If you've upset her with your stories . . .'

'I haven't!'

She straightened up. 'Good. Otherwise we can't look after you,' she said. 'Do you understand?'

She eyed the bags in her daughters' hands then looked at Uncle Vaughn. 'Did they need quite so much?' She tutted. 'I shouldn't have left you in charge.' Then she pulled her handbag over her shoulder. 'Girls!'

Fliss jumped then she and Kitty followed Aunt Cece without saying anything about me or showing off their shopping, which definitely wasn't normal Kitty and Fliss behaviour. I shuffled my feet in the awkward Aunt-Cece-shaped space and waited for Uncle Vaughn to say something. I looked up the stairs and crossed my legs to stop myself running back up. He sighed heavily, rubbed his temples, then slapped his jolly face back on.

'Try not to worry,' he said, ruffling my hair. 'I'll have a word with her.' He gave me a small smile then, handed me a white carrier bag. 'Some clothes for you. Just like Kitty and Fliss.' He winked. 'On the credit card, so hush, hush, all right?'

He opened his mouth as if he was going to say something else, but my aunt shouted, 'Vaughn!' and we both jumped.

With raised eyebrows he followed his family out to the guesthouse.

I let out a breath. Her words picked at me. '*Otherwise we can't look after you.*' As if she'd been doing that already. As if she was Mum of the Year.

I shook my head and peered into the white bag at the folded clothes. There was a fair amount of pink and everything looked stretchy. I closed the bag, sighing, and leant it against the staircase post. It was nice of Uncle Vaughn to buy me something – at least he was making an effort – but did it have to be so pink?

I heard a sniff and turned to the front door to see a pink leg, a darker pink arm, and a load of plastic bags.

'Fliss?'

Another sniff, then Fliss leant into the side of the door as if she was glued to it.

'Are you all right?' I asked.

She nodded, then burst into tears and ran towards me.

'It's . . . it's . . . it's . . .'

Her breath hitched and with every inhalation her shoulders lifted and the bags in her arms swished and crinkled. I stood there for a second, then guided her to the bottom of the stairs and sat her down.

'It's just . . . it's so awful,' she said between sobs.

I patted her on the shoulder, but carefully, as though she might turn rabid at any moment.

'I overheard them talking,' she sniffed. 'It was late and I couldn't sleep and I heard them arguing again. Mum said Dad had lost all our money, and we'd lose the house, and he has to move out after the holiday, and they're going to get a divorce, and everything is ruined forever.'

She dissolved into noisy sobs but didn't let go of her bags.

I didn't know what to say. It was a bit of a shock though Aunt Cece had never seemed to like Uncle Vaughn very much. I carried on patting Fliss's arm.

'So I asked them and Mum says we'll sort everything out after the holiday.' She stared at her shopping bags. 'But I just want my family back,' she sobbed.

I dropped my hand from her shoulder. 'I know what you mean.'

Fliss looked up at me through red eyes and blotchy, puffed cheeks. 'Sorry, Angela. I didn't mean, I mean . . . I know I'm lucky really.'

And with that she started crying again.

'Fliss!'

My head snapped up; Fliss's followed. Standing in the doorway was Kitty, one hand on her hip.

'What are you doing?'

'Nothing,' Fliss said, wiping her nose and eyes on her sleeve. 'I was showing Angela my clothes.'

She turned to me and I nodded.

'Yeah. They're, erm, lovely,' I said, shrugging.

Kitty narrowed her eyes. 'Mum's waiting,' she said.

Fliss stood up, gathering her rustling bags.

'*Now*, Fliss,' Kitty said, as if she'd been kept waiting hours.

'Thanks,' Fliss whispered out of the corner of her mouth, and without a backward glance, she picked up all the bags, including mine, and followed her sister.

I sat on the stairs for a while until it dawned on me that I'd totally got away with being upstairs, but with it I'd nearly lost my chance of staying with them. But what about the divorce and Uncle Vaughn losing all their money? I couldn't live with my aunt and uncle if they weren't even living together.

I rubbed my eyes. Who cared about my aunt and uncle, anyway? But then I thought about Fliss confiding in me and even saying thanks, and Uncle Vaughn buying me clothes, even if they were the last clothes on earth I'd want to wear. Maybe it could work. I bit my lip. I really didn't want to go to a new kids' home. Maybe they'd let me stay, whatever happened, if I did exactly what my aunt told me to.

But what about Julien? If I did what Aunt Cece said, I'd be leaving him to die.

I looked up the stairs. He felt more important than anything she could say or do. I had to help him and for that, I'd need Herman.

I found him in the kitchen. Armuth was nowhere to be seen, but judging by the banging coming from the annexe I suspected she was in there.

'Herman,' I said, with a side look at the annexe door to make sure it stayed shut, 'can I use the salon? I need some books about the house – about its history.' I took a deep breath. 'And the boy. Please?'

Herman's eyebrows bunched together, forming one of his piercing stares. It made my skin prickle, as if he was searching through my thoughts one by one. I tried to stand a little taller.

He bowed his head and his face seemed to droop.

'I'd feel better if I had permission,' I said, thinking of Aunt Cece.

When he didn't say anything I carried on.

'I'll be really careful. I won't break anything, I promise, and I'll be out of there before anyone else finds out.'

The thumping stopped and we both turned towards the annexe. He had to say it was okay before Armuth came back. I didn't want to upset her again.

'Please, Herman,' I said quietly, 'it's life and death.'

Chapter Twenty-Six

From the annexe came a sound of crashing pots and pans. Herman slowly turned to me and nodded.

'Thanks, Herman,' I said, and followed him out of the kitchen.

To my surprise he ignored the salon, taking me straight to the library – the out of bounds library! As soon as I opened the door I was blasted by the smell of damp. It wasn't a large room and looked smaller because of the old wooden bookcases along each wall from floor to ceiling. Mould like pale green and grey flowers sprouted across their glass fronts. Most of the cases were unlocked; their doors hanging open like hungry mouths, the books inside like rotten holey teeth. Piles of large, heavy-looking books had been left in the middle of the room, half covered by dustsheets. Under the largest dustsheet lump I found a desk and chair made of the same wood as the bathroom.

I turned to Herman and he pretended to crack something against the table and eat it. I thought about the orchard where I'd kicked the small stones.

'Walnuts!'

Herman nodded.

I grinned then scuffed the floor with my shoes. Bits of frayed carpet stuck to my trainers. 'You won't tell, will you?' I said. 'I mean, please don't tell anyone that I'm in here. Aunt Cece wouldn't get it.'

I looked up, but Herman had gone.

I turned to the books. I pulled the left window shutter open for more light and then, because I had to start somewhere, picked a book at random from the nearest shelf, then another and another. They were all written in French. I sighed. I should've realised they'd all be in French.

At first I looked for anything with the name of the house in the title, but after two walls I'd found nothing. I was on the third when a set of three books caught my eye, all bearing the title, *Maison de Noyer – Une histoire des environs*.

'*Histoire*. History? Yes!'

The books were a warm, deep red colour, with the title picked out in a gold that flaked off on my fingers. I pulled out the first one and it was so heavy the book opened itself in the middle, yellowed paper crisping into two sections. I ran a finger down the uneven brown-tinged edges then tried to read some of it, but each page was filled with rows and rows of tight black type in horrible and impossible French.

I lifted out all three books and carried them to the table. They hit it with a whump and stirred up a cloud of dust, which I waved away. The first book was useless, filled with a ridiculously long list of numbers, so I set it aside. The second seemed to be a history because the chapter titles had dates. I thumbed through to the section that included 1898. The first few lines talked about the son of the son of the son, but the word 'son' was pretty much the only word I understood because it reminded me of my dad's name, Phil, so that wasn't much help.

I sighed and more dust swirled.

I picked up the last book. This one creaked open. It was filled with dates and lists of births, marriages and deaths. I shivered. Deaths . . . There had to be something useful in this one.

I tried to be careful, but shook with excitement as I flicked towards the end of the book. It ran empty though, the pages blank. I checked the front, running a shaking finger down the list of names and dates beginning in the 1750s. I flipped faster and faster through the book counting upwards as I reached the late 1800s. Julien had to be here – he had to!

The numbers rose rapidly as I got closer to the end of the century. There were lots of complicated words I couldn't understand, but hundreds and hundreds of dates of deaths, which I did.

I gripped the book.

My eyes flicked to a note at the bottom of the page, which led to another page with a list of villages I recognised from the drive to the house. I traced the names with my finger and felt something under the page. I pulled at it and a piece of paper fluttered to the floor. I picked it up and discovered a pretty hand-drawn map of the house and land, as it must have looked years ago. But once I worked out the shaded areas were massive burial grounds, it wasn't quite so nice. And the hundreds of little crosses littering the space around the left and front of the house had to be the graveyard.

I turned the map over, but there was nothing there. I looked back in the book but the following pages were all blank. No one had written in it after August,1898. I picked up the first book again and checked the back. That too was blank. I flicked through it carefully, realising it was an accounts book, with lists of numbers on each page and totals at the bottom, just like the ones my dad worked on really, but older. Like the other books, there was nothing in it after 1898. I remembered Armuth had said something about each generation trying to keep the house going and I shivered. 1898 was when it all started to go wrong. 1898 is when all those people died. So why couldn't I find Julien's name?

I thumped the book shut.

'Oops, sorry,' I said, smoothing the book, and giving it a little pat.

'It's okay,' someone said back, and I spun round to find Fliss standing right behind me.

Chapter Twenty-Seven

I was trying to stop hyperventilating and come up with an excuse for being in the library at the same time when Fliss leant past me and picked up the third book, which I'd left open.

'Wow, so many deaths that year,' she said, looking from the map to the history book, then pointing to the long list of deaths. 'From typhoid, it says here. *T* stands for *Typhoïde*.'

I frowned, ready to deny anything she said, then I broke into a grin as I flicked through the pages. 'Can you read this?'

Fliss nodded. 'Yes,' she said, 'it says the whole place was . . .' She paused, reading. 'See here?' She traced the words with fluorescent pink nails. 'Oh it was bad, really bad. It says here that all the surrounding villages were destroyed. Everything, all of it gone.'

She stared at the picture. 'Oh look, the house used to be bigger.'

Fliss pointed to the left-hand side of the drawing. Next to Julien's room was a tower and a whole heap of other rooms that didn't exist now. My jaw dropped. That had to be where the servant was coming from.

Fliss had turned back to the original list, running a finger over the complicated words. To me they seemed to run into each other, but this was a whole new side to Fliss and it made me think. Maybe she wasn't all about pink leggings and following everything Kitty said.

'Everyone in the house got sick,' she said. 'It looks like they all died. Hang on.'

With a neon nail holding her place, she loosened a piece of yellowed paper, tissue-thin. It looked like a page from a newspaper.

'Oh!'

She spread the paper out over the book. I leant closer. There was a drawing of a stern-looking bearded man and the house. The rest was all in French.

'What does it say, Fliss? Who's that?'

'Nicolas Brodeur. He was the only one left. He inherited the house when the young master, Julien Bastien, died.'

I gasped and took a step back, but she didn't seem to notice. I tried to get my mouth to ask how he died, but Fliss spoke first.

'There was a fire,' she said, following the tiny type with her nail, but being careful not to break the paper. 'A whole side of the house was burnt and loads of the grounds and the villages nearby.'

The sun dipped behind a cloud and the light in the library dimmed. Fliss's words hung in the air as she looked at the empty bookcases then at the floor, anywhere but at me. I dug my nails into my palms.

The dinner bell shattered the silence.

'Look, I'm sorry,' Fliss began, winding her hair round her hand. 'I didn't mean anything, about the fire. It's just what it says.'

The bell rang again, but neither of us moved.

Fliss looked at the books on the table. 'Why are you so interested in all this, anyway?'

'No reason,' I said.

Fliss cocked her head to one side and I could tell she knew there was more to this. 'I'm sorry,' she said. 'About . . . you know . . . stuff.'

'Yeah. And thanks,' I mumbled, nodding to the books, 'for, all this.'

She hovered, switching from one foot to the other, one hand inside her jacket. The dinner bell rang again, but I didn't move and neither did she.

Suddenly she rushed towards me and pressed some papers into my hand.

'I think you should have this. It's in French and I can't understand it all, but I found them . . .' She looked behind her then back at me. 'They were in Mum's handbag.' She kept glancing at the door. 'Don't tell. Just take a look, okay?' She ran to the door. 'Then put them back!'

'Wait! Fliss?'

But she'd gone. I was about to take a look at the papers when the dinner bell rang again. I didn't want to get into trouble, so I shoved them down the back of my leggings, but then I had a thought.

Julien said his uncle told him it would be the end of everything if anyone knew he was up there. Fliss had read that nearly everyone had died of typhoid, and then there was the fire. I thought back to Julien.

'*They will burn the houses,*' he'd said. '*If people are sick, they will burn them and anything or anyone inside them.*'

I shivered.

What if people had heard about the sickness here, and came to burn the house?

The bell rang for the fifth time. I threw a dustsheet over the books.

If I closed my eyes I could see Julien's pale face, hear his rattling cough. I thought of all the little crosses on the hand-drawn map. I thought of a fire raging and him stuck in his room. I couldn't let him die like that. I had to help him. I had to change the past.

The library fell away. I screwed my eyes tight as the nightmare slithered into my thoughts. I felt a wall of heat pressing against my face.

'Daddy!'

Suddenly I was snatched back and shaken hard. I flung my arms out to fight them off, but when I opened my eyes it wasn't a fireman, it was Aunt Cece shaking me, pinpoints of red on each cheek. No flames, no fire – and on top of everything, she'd caught me in the library. The papers down my back crinkled. I thought of what Fliss said about taking them from her mum's handbag. There was no way she'd let me stay if she found them on me. I let my arms drop to my side.

Once she realised she'd got my attention Aunt Cece let go and straightened her skirt. Only then did I realise what she had under her other arm: my sewing box. I felt anger boiling inside my chest. She'd been in my room and touched my things!

Her lips curved up at the edges into a smile so fixed it looked painful.

'I've been speaking to Armuth.' She paused for a dramatic breath. 'I think you'd better explain where you got this.'

I stuck out my chin. 'From the kitchen cupboard.'

Her right eye twitched. 'Don't play smart with me, young lady,' she said, still smiling that horrible smile.

'I'm not,' I said, 'that's where I got it.'

'No stories now, Angela.'

My eyes began to prickle, which made me even more angry. 'I'm not,' I said. 'Herman said I could have it. It's the truth. I haven't done anything wrong!'

'Herman?'

'Yes!'

'Armuth's husband?'

Her eyebrows lifted so high I thought they'd jump off her face.

'Yes!'

She put a hand across her forehead as if I was giving her a headache. 'Angela, what on earth are you talking about?' Her voice was sickly sweet.

'He did,' I shouted at her. 'He said it was for me!'

'Stop it, Angela!'

She bent towards me. Her nasty smile was gone and in its place was a cold, hard stare. Behind her I glimpsed Armuth hovering in the hallway. She looked perplexed, her gaze moving between my aunt and me.

'Angela,' Aunt Cece said through her teeth. 'Herman died years ago.'

She paused, gave a half turn as if she knew Armuth was behind her then turned back to me, lowering her voice.

'He was broken-hearted after . . . well, he was broken-hearted.'

I shook my head. It was impossible. Herman wasn't dead. He couldn't be. How could I have been talking to a dead person?

I thought back to us making hot chocolate and, later on, Herman giving me the sewing box. He was real – as real as Aunt Cece, as real as Armuth.

'But he did give it to me,' I began, then looked at Aunt Cece's face. Something in her expression sent shivers down my spine. This wasn't a joke.

But Herman dead? Herman a ghost? I shook my head. It couldn't be true.

'He did give it to me,' I told them, my voice almost a whisper, my legs starting to feel like jelly. 'He did, I promise.'

Armuth dropped her gaze. Aunt Cece turned and saw, and her voice hardened.

'Now look what you've done. These silly stories you make up actually hurt people. How could you? I mean it's one thing frightening the other children in the home, but deliberately upsetting Armuth?' She shook her head. 'Go to your room and stay there.'

But before I could move, she pinched a corner of my blouse. 'And you can put this back as well.' She shook her head slowly, clicking her teeth. 'Taking what's not yours. You should know better. *My* girls know better.'

Before I could stop them, angry, hot sobs spilt over my cheeks. This was the Aunt Cece I knew, the one Mum had hated, in person, at last. How could I have even thought about trying to live with her? I barged past her and ran to my room.

'You see what I mean, Armuth?' Aunt Cece trilled behind me. 'I try my best, but she's a lot of work.' She lowered her voice, but I could still hear. 'I was the only one prepared to take her in, you know.'

I slammed the door then stood back as the whole thing creaked on its hinges. I threw myself onto the cot and screamed with frustration into the pillow, treacherous tears soaking the cover. I hated her! I hated her! And she was the liar, not me. Herman had given it to me, he had. Ghost or not.

Chapter Twenty-Eight

I cried until I started to hiccup. Then I gulped air and ran over Aunt Cece's words in my head, back through all the conversations and everything that had happened here in France, and realised that no one had ever mentioned Herman – no one at all, apart from me. Well, me and Armuth. Thinking about it now, she'd never laid a plate out for him at dinner; he never ate with us, even though he sometimes sat at the table. I realised that I'd never actually heard him speak, but I thought that was because of his throat. I thought there was something wrong with it. But then, I'd never heard his footsteps either. He just seemed to be there. I thought about how he was always pointing at things, never touching them. He hadn't made me hot chocolate, he'd got me to open the fridge and make it myself. But I wasn't lying, not about this, which meant only one thing. Herman really was a ghost.

I shivered.

I thought about how he'd been so kind and how he'd helped me, showing me the library and everything. He was the only one. Armuth was nice enough and she seemed like she wanted to say something to me whenever we were on our own, but she never did. Now she'd think I was making up stories about her dead husband, so that was the end of that. And after saying I'd seen Herman, Aunt Cece would definitely be telling Mrs Morrison she didn't want me.

'*I was the only one prepared to take her in.*'

Past tense.

My shoulders slumped.

It wasn't fair. I'd tried to like them. I'd tried to fit in and get them to like me. I hadn't made Herman up. I'd seen him. I'd spoken to him. And no one believed me.

I sniffed and looked around the room, as if he might appear at any moment. I rubbed my arms, suddenly feeling really cold. A bubble of panic started to work its way up my throat. What would I do if he turned up right now? I could scream, but Aunt Cece would think I was making it up. Apparently no one else could see him. I tugged the sleeves of my blouse down, then touched the tiny stitches I'd made only the night before. Herman had given me the sewing box and he'd said I could use the clothes in the cupboard. It wasn't the first time he'd helped me. I thought about how Aunt Cece had done nothing but the opposite, and blew out a breath, shook myself and let the panic go. Herman might be a ghost and that might be totally weird and really spooky, but he was a hundred times nicer than she was. If it came to it, I'd trust his ghost over her any day.

The papers I'd shoved down my back crackled. I turned over, pulled them out and grinned when I saw they were the same old papers Herman had been reading on the dresser, but less crinkled, newer looking. I saw my dad's name again, but the rest of the French was difficult to read and the print on this copy dense. I turned the first page over.

Fliss had said I should take a look, maybe she'd seen my dad's name too, but I couldn't understand any of it and there was no chance of getting her to translate when she was probably hanging out with Kitty and I was stuck in my room. I threw the papers on the bed – then snatched them back. Of course! Julien could read them for me. I just had to get upstairs without being seen.

I folded the papers as small as possible and snuck to the door. I reached for the handle, but before I got to it there was a knock.

The door swung open as I stuffed the papers down the back of my leggings again.

Kitty smoothed her ponytail. 'We're letting you out

for dinner,' she giggled. 'But not for good behaviour, apparently.'

She raised her eyebrows then looked me up and down. 'I know something you don't know,' she said. 'Something you're not supposed to know.' She paused. 'But I might tell you, if you ask nicely.'

A smile spread across her face and I could see why people thought she was pretty.

'Look,' I said, 'I don't want any dinner and I don't care what you have to say, so you can just go.'

'Oo-ooh,' she said, her eyes shining.

I waited.

She fluttered her eyelashes.

'What, Kitty?'

'Guess,' she said.

I rolled my eyes.

'Guess!'

'Look, I don't care,' I said and tried to shut the door, but she put her foot in the way.

'You're not going to live with us!' she sang, tossing her hair like a pony in a competition.

I took a deep breath. I'd known this was coming. Somewhere inside I'd always known this was coming. But it still stung.

'You really did it this time with your stories. Congratulations,' she said, grinding a fake electric blue nail down the edge of the door. Strips of old paint flaked to the floor.

She stared at me, but I couldn't speak. I kept swallowing, but my mouth felt dry.

Kitty snorted. 'I mean, no one's going to say anything yet, but I overheard Mum talking.' She flicked more paint off the door. Tiny flakes landed on my top. 'And she said it wouldn't be good for us. You know, for Fliss and me.'

I seemed to be blinking really fast.

She screwed her face up in mock pity. 'You know, what with seeing ghosts, lying all the time and upsetting Armuth? She said you're a bad influence.'

I felt the roar and rush of something fierce and hot fill me from my shoes up. So they didn't want me? So what? I didn't want them either. I didn't want anything here, not any more.

'Now I know you won't tell Mum that you know because you don't want to upset her, do you? I mean, maybe there's still time for her to change her mind.'

I tried to swallow my anger back down.

'And you wouldn't want to get me into trouble for saying anything, would you?'

I clenched my fists, and Kitty watched my hands.

'Because I might be able to help. I could have a word with Mum. Maybe, if I felt like it. Then you wouldn't have to go to a mouldy old children's home, would you?'

She put on a fake sad face, but when I didn't say anything she tossed her ponytail.

'Well, you have a think about it,' she said, adding, 'Oh, and so will I.' Then she smiled and flounced off down the hallway.

I wanted to scream and punch the pillows, tear the cot apart, pull the wardrobe over – even punch Kitty.

Instead I kicked the cot.

'An-ge-la?' Kitty's voice echoed down the corridor. 'Din-ner!'

I took off the blouse, hung it back in the wardrobe and shut the door on it. I shrugged on a dark green pinafore dress with a long-sleeved T-shirt I'd sewn into it and pockets I'd crocheted on the front, over my leggings. I added a navy blue woolly cardigan that came down to my knees over the top. Then I followed Kitty.

In the kitchen everyone was talking over the top of each other, but it all felt a bit too loud. Uncle Vaughn was wearing his 'I'm so cheerful' face and Kitty and Fliss laughed at his jokes, but they were just as lame as always. Aunt Cece's grin was fixed as she looked around the kitchen and made notes in a small pad at the side of her plate.

I could feel the papers against my back. There was no way I was leaving them in my room, not now Aunt

Cece had been snooping. I felt a small smile growing, just knowing they were there, with my dad's name on them, but then I noticed everyone round the table was staring at me, and laughing.

'It's very sad, really,' Kitty was telling her dad. 'It's like she *wants* to look like a homeless person.'

She looked at me and mouthed her next words. 'Changed my mind. Loser.'

I looked down. One of my cardigan sleeves was fraying and the left side pocket had come loose on my dress. I itched to rip it off and start again.

Suddenly Fliss cleared her throat. 'Can you tell us a bit more about the history of the house, Armuth? Only Angela has a lot of questions about its history, don't you, Angela?'

I glared at Fliss, wondering if this was a trick, if she was going to say something mean, but that was all she said. I didn't dare look at Aunt Cece. Herman had his head in his hands. My heart stopped for a second. Herman!

But I didn't have time to think because all eyes, bar his, were on me. The silence grew longer. I felt as if the floor was moving under my feet.

'It's just . . .' I said, willing Herman to look up, willing everyone else to see him, '. . . we've been studying it at school,' I said, trying to come up with a story so they wouldn't know I'd been snooping in the library. 'About

– 168 –

typhoid, I mean, and I wanted to ask if . . .'

Aunt Cece gave such a sharp intake of breath her mouth actually made an 'o' shape. Uncle Vaughn coughed loudly. Kitty and Fliss stared from one parent to the other until Armuth, who'd gone white, placed her knife and fork on her untouched plate and stood. I flinched as her chair scraped along the floor.

Aunt Cece rose up too. 'Armuth, I'm so, so sorry,' she said.

But with a sad look at Herman, Armuth walked out.

I gasped. Armuth had looked at him. She'd seen him. She knew he was there!

I was about to call after her when I noticed Aunt Cece was staring at me, her lips pursed so tightly together I thought she might burst. She nodded once to Kitty and Fliss.

'Girls. Out. Now.'

'What's the matter with Armuth?' Kitty said.

'But I haven't finished my dinner,' Fliss said, already pocketing roast potatoes.

'We are so close,' Aunt Cece said to Uncle Vaughn. 'So close.' She pointed at me. 'How could you upset Armuth? Again!' She snatched her hand back. 'It's as if you're deliberately trying to ruin everything.'

I opened my mouth to speak, but she carried on.

'I won't let you. I've worked too hard.' She brushed

the edge of the old stove with her fingertips then picked up her notepad. 'You don't deserve any of this.'

Then she ushered her girls out.

I felt like sweeping everything off the table, imagined hearing the satisfying smash of plates breaking into tiny pieces and cutlery clanging against the stone floor, all the uneaten food mushed underfoot.

Nobody wanted me, not my aunt, not the kids' home, not any kids' home. They all moved me on. I was just another problem. I'd be more welcome in 1898 with Julien than with anyone here. I bit my lip. Suddenly that didn't seem such a ridiculous idea. What if I didn't go back to the home? What if I found a new home – with Julien? It wasn't like I had anything to lose.

I speared a potato with my fork and pushed it from one side of my plate to the other. I'd wait till they'd all gone to bed then I'd creep upstairs. And I wouldn't come back. Ever.

Chapter Twenty-Nine

Uncle Vaughn was concentrating on his plate of food, but I nudged his elbow, then inclined my head to where Herman was sitting.

'What, Angela?'

I turned to Herman, but he got up and followed Armuth out to the annexe. My uncle didn't see a thing and went back to his dinner.

I stared at the slowly congealing duck fat yellowing on my plate and my stomach rolled. I put my cutlery together without taking another bite, just as my uncle finished his. The last ten minutes didn't seem to have affected his appetite.

He patted his growing paunch and swivelled round in his chair. 'Look, Angela,' he said. 'I'm really not sure why you mentioned it.'

'What?'

'Typhoid.' He frowned. 'Armuth and Herman's son? He died of typhoid.'

'What?' I gasped, shifting to the edge of my seat, one leg kicking against the table leg.

'Yes, he was young, in his twenties. Poor boy.'

My leg stilled. I felt awful for upsetting Armuth, but this was huge. I had to know more.

He leant back in his chair. 'You really didn't know?'

I shook my head. 'What happened?'

'He worked in the Congo – mining, I think. There was an outbreak and they wanted him brought home.' His eyes softened. 'So they treated him here and, well, he died.'

I grabbed the edge of the table, my foot tapped against the floor and my brain fizzed with thoughts. Their son had typhoid and they'd treated him in the house! They must have had medicines. This could help Julien! This could save him!

I had a gazillion questions and the first one burst out before I could think. 'With what?'

'Hmmmm?' Uncle Vaughn had started to collect the abandoned plates.

'You said they treated him here,' I said. 'How?'

He turned from the sink with plates and bowls balanced precariously in his arms. I noticed two of his shirt buttons had burst.

'You're a curious girl, aren't you?' he said, raising his eyebrows.

I shrugged.

'Well,' he said, 'with antibiotics, I suppose.' He turned back to the sink, dunking the plates and bowls in with a worrying clash.

'But what sort?' I said, getting up to help.

He extracted a plate with a large new chip in it and swore under his breath. 'Hmmm? Oh, I don't know, Angela. Some sort of penicillin.' He put the chipped plate on the draining board. 'Are you finished, because I'll wash yours.'

I passed it over. My stomach rumbled, but I only had to look at the film of fat on the plate to feel sick again.

'Where exactly did he die?' I said.

He sighed. 'What? Look, can you empty that in the bin?'

I scraped away the meat, gristle and fat, then handed the plate back. 'Where exactly? What room?'

Uncle Vaughn was up to his elbows in bubbles because he'd used too much washing-up liquid. He swore again then grimaced. 'Don't repeat that to your aunt!'

I hopped from foot to foot and tried not to scream with frustration as he washed the last of the dishes and dried his hands before answering.

'Listen, Angela. It doesn't matter because it must have

been too late for the treatment to work.' He put the drying-up cloth on the range. 'That's why upstairs is out of bounds, I expect.' He ruffled my hair. 'But there's no house ghost, whatever Armuth said. So there's no need to worry, eh?'

But I wasn't worried. My mind was racing. If they treated their son here then they might still have some of the medicine left. I could give it to Julien and he'd get better. I just needed to know where to look.

The shutters above the sink rattled, breathing a cold breeze through the kitchen. I shivered and turned towards them.

Uncle Vaughn laughed. His jolly face was back. 'You can't catch typhoid here, you know,' he said.

He waited for me to join in the joke, but I was looking round the kitchen, wondering where Armuth kept her medicines.

He took a deep breath. 'Angela, you're not really worried about things like ghosts, are you, eh?' When I didn't reply, he cleared his throat and shuffled a little. 'You see, when people die, it can be hard to imagine them gone, but . . .'

'I've got a headache!' I said. I didn't want to think about what he was going to say.

Uncle Vaughn frowned, then steepled his fingers against his lips.

'Perhaps there's a first-aid box in the house?' I said.

'Ah.' He looked round the kitchen. 'I'm not sure and I think we'd better leave Armuth alone for the moment.'

My cheeks flushed, thinking about upsetting her, but she knew something. I would swear she'd looked at Herman at the table.

'We'll ask your aunt,' he said suddenly, putting his arm round me.

'What?'

He grinned.

'She's got everything you could possibly need in that handbag of hers.'

I remembered Fliss telling me she'd taken the papers from her mum's handbag. That was the last place I wanted Aunt Cece to look.

'No, it's okay. I'm fine. Really,' I said. 'My headache's going now and I probably just need a good night's sleep.'

But my excuses didn't work and he marched me out of the kitchen.

Chapter Thirty

Stepping out of the back door, I could see the outline of the guesthouse. Tiny insects buzzed around the old porch light lit against the darkening grey-purple sky. We crossed the gravel, I felt cobbles under my feet and smelt a pile of chopped wood, then I followed Uncle Vaughn over a small bridge. He unlocked a gate and rapped at the door, but when no one answered, he opened it himself, holding the door for me. I gnawed at my thumbnail and reluctantly stepped in.

It was warm inside with old, thick rugs on the floor and a radiator belching out so much heat everything above it was hazy, but there was a sharp smell of new paint and the plastic draped over two armchairs and a dining table set reminded me that the house was for sale.

Aunt Cece was lifting the cushions of a battered old sofa. She looked up as we walked in and her face dropped.

'Just come for some paracetamol for Angela,' Uncle Vaughn said.

'I'm fine, really,' I said, but they weren't listening.

Aunt Cece stood and they whispered at each other.

I hovered near the main window, looking at the objects left on the sill: a small wicker horse and a lump of metal I wasn't sure was anything at all.

Then Uncle Vaughn spoke up. He sounded weary. 'It doesn't seem right,' he said.

'You agreed, remember?' Aunt Cece snapped. 'And I've offered Armuth more money.'

She whispered the next bit and I missed it, but I wondered about that. If Fliss was right and Uncle Vaughn had lost all their money, how come Aunt Cece was offering more to Armuth. And why was she giving money to Armuth in the first place? She got louder again.

'She'll be thinking about it. We just need her to sign.' There was a pause, then she added, 'You're not going to back out now. I mean, it's not really for me, remember, it's for the girls – their future. You owe it to us. You lost us one house. I won't let you lose another one.'

Thunder rumbled above us, close and heavy. They didn't seem to notice as Aunt Cece continued, 'The girls need more than a few bags of clothes paid for on your credit cards!'

A few seconds later rain fell in sheets onto the thin roof.

'And someone has to clear up your mess.'

Then I heard my name. It was Uncle Vaughn.

'Perhaps Angela could stay with you girls here then, just for tonight. It can't be that much fun for her over in the big house.'

'No!' I said, thinking out loud.

'No,' Aunt Cece said, at the same time.

Her eyes widened as if she'd realised I was still there. 'I mean, you're fine in the big house, aren't you?' She looked at me, smiled her best fake smile, then lowered her voice. 'And I need to find my copy of the papers.'

I froze and turned back to the window.

In the reflection I watched her rummage through her handbag, then give some pills to Uncle Vaughn.

'I thought they were in here, but I must have put them in the bedroom. I need to look.' She picked up her bag and stalked out the room.

I took the pills from him, put them in my half torn off pocket, then pulled my cardigan over my head. When I reached the door I realised my uncle was following.

'It's okay, Uncle Vaughn. I know the way back.'

'Yes, yes, yes,' he said, reaching for a large umbrella leaning against the wall. He fumbled with the automatic catch, then closed and opened the umbrella two more times. He looked behind him, sighed, then picked up a bag I hadn't noticed on my way in. He gave me a small, sad smile.

'Well, then, let's go, eh?'

We hurried across the slick cobbles onto the gravel as the rain showered down. It was awkward under the umbrella with him so much taller than me and trying to keep his bag dry at the same time. Rumbles of thunder banged so close overhead they shook my bones and made my ribs hum.

Suddenly the wind turned the umbrella inside out. I was drenched in seconds, but couldn't help giggling at him wrestling with it. He swore, without apologising this time, and I laughed even louder. He looked like he was trying to wrestle a large, disobedient bat.

'Get indoors, Angela,' he shouted and I turned, still laughing, to run in, but the porch light was out and the door locked.

'We'll have to go round the front,' I shouted back.

Uncle Vaughn nodded, still struggling with the umbrella. I ran round the side, hunching over, but the wind pulled at my cardigan and rain slid down my neck.

'Angela?'

I turned to him then ducked, squeezing my eyes shut as a flash of lightning hit the top of the house. I looked up and that's when I saw a thin, flickering light just where the lightning had hit. The rain soaked me to the skin as I counted the windows from the centre of the house to the left-hand side.

One, two, three, four, five, six, seven, eight, nine. Nine!

It was Julien's window and there was another next to it!

Lightning flashed again and I saw the tower, the missing wing – and a face!

'Julien,' I said.

'Angela?'

I spun round. Uncle Vaughn had fixed the umbrella and was holding it over me.

'What is it? What's the matter?'

He stared up at the house and I looked back too, except there was nothing to see now. It was so dark you could barely see the outline of the house and the rain poured as if someone was emptying a jug over us. It was completely dark; no light and no face.

Uncle Vaughn hurried me along and kept up a steady chatter as we splashed through the gravel and into the house. He kept shooting me funny looks, but I ignored him.

'Now then, eh?' he said, stopping outside my bedroom door. 'You dry off and get a good night's rest. And don't you worry about anything.' He winked. 'I'm just next door.'

I froze.

'And I promise to ward off any ghosts, okay?'

He pretended to sword-fight, which stung because it was the kind of thing my dad would do. The kind of thing my dad would've done.

I dripped on the floor. He stopped play-fighting.

'Your aunt is trying her best, you know.'

I fiddled with the paracetamol in my pocket.

'I'm not an easy man to live with.' He chuckled. 'Spent far too much again.' He scratched his head. 'Don't suppose you've got a spare tenner in that pocket, have you?'

I looked up and he laughed.

'Well, good night, Angela.'

Once I shut my door I heard him shuffle next door just like he'd said. The shutters flapped in the wind. I looked at the ceiling as if I could see through it to the mirror upstairs and beyond that to Julien. It was now or never. Uncle or no uncle, ghosts or no ghosts, I was going to help him. I was going to look for the medicines.

Chapter Thirty-One

With one ear trained on the wall between Uncle Vaughn's room and mine, I peeled off my wet clothes and slipped into the only other clean things I could find: my jean shorts, cardigan and T-shirt. My tights were still laddered and baggy at the knees but at least they were warm.

I squeezed out my hair and put it up in a rough ponytail. It would be wild and tangled tomorrow, but I wouldn't be around for Aunt Cece to say anything. I grinned for what felt like the first time in ages.

The house creaked around me, the rain pelted steadily against the window and the shutters flapped back and forth. I wrapped myself in some of the blankets, hugging them round me for warmth.

Finally I heard snoring. I threw the blankets onto the nearest cot then turned the handle of my bedroom door and lifted it up to avoid any squeaking. Leaving it ajar, I crept along the corridor.

I passed the suit of armour, sliding heel-toe, heel-toe in the dark until I heard something that stopped me cold. It was a strange, snuffling noise that sounded more animal than human. I shuddered, thinking of rats and mice. Then the snuffling turned into a low moan. I turned around, looking longingly down the corridor towards my room, but I didn't move. The medicines had to be here somewhere.

The moan turned back into snuffling. I took a deep breath and edged closer. The noise was coming from the salon. If I was going to try the kitchen or upstairs to look for medicines, I'd have to pass it. I tiptoed closer, hugging the walls. The snuffling got louder and louder until I was clutching the edge of the door. I took another breath then forced myself to look.

But it wasn't mice or rats or even a ghost. It was much, much worse. It was Armuth.

She was weeping, an old photo album spread across her lap. I realised they had to be photos of Herman and her son. Her dead husband and their son, the one I'd reminded her about earlier. I drew back and sagged against the wall.

Uncle Vaughn had said it wasn't my fault, but I felt the hot stinging twist of guilt and sorrow all tangled up together inside of me. I stared at my feet and when I looked up again I had to stifle a scream as Herman's face loomed out of the dark.

Armuth's chair creaked. The snuffling stopped. Had she heard me?

My mouth flapped open and shut as I tried to come up with an excuse for what could only be seen as my spying on Armuth. Then I realised I was seeing Herman, except he was dead! I pressed my back into the wall as if I could melt into it, but he put a finger to his lips and drew me away. I followed slowly, thinking, 'But he's a ghost. He's a ghost,' over and over in my head. The snuffling started up again behind us.

'I'm sorry,' I whispered, once we were further down the corridor. 'I wasn't spying, I promise. I was just looking for medicines.'

Herman turned and frowned.

'I didn't mean to upset Armuth. I didn't know about your son. I'm really sorry, Herman.'

He narrowed his eyes. I could barely see the rest of him in the dark.

'I really am,' I whispered.

He beckoned for me to follow, but to my surprise he turned away from the kitchen and, checking I was still behind him, began to walk up the main stairs.

I paused.

'Herman? Are you really a ghost?'

But Herman had faded into the darkness.

I longed to follow, but Armuth was only a few steps away. She gave another low moan and I shivered, rubbing the tops of my arms. I stared after Herman, reminding myself that he might be a ghost, but he'd helped me before and I could probably trust him. With a quick look back at the salon, I followed him upstairs.

Chapter Thirty-Two

Herman was waiting for me on the first floor. He pointed to the door on my left, nodded once then turned away.

'Wait – Herman?'

But he'd already gone.

The wind sighed and so did I. I had so many questions for him and not just about him being a real, proper ghost. Herman had to have a reason for bringing me up here. My eyes strayed up to where I knew Julien would be. I'd mentioned medicines to Herman. Was he trying to help me? Did he know something?

I opened the door he'd pointed to a few centimetres, then a few more. My hand tightened on the doorknob.

The slats across the windows were in a worse state than anywhere else in the house. There were large gaps between each one, warped apart by the weather. The moonlight shining through made prison bars of light across the floor. I thought of Julien trapped in his room, and stepped inside.

There was a neatly made single bed and a bedside table. On top of that was a candle stub in a round metal holder and a box of matches by its side.

I wiped my damp palms against my tights, picked up the matches and struck one against the box. It sizzled brightly before snuffling out, as if someone had blown on it. I looked behind me.

'Who's there?'

My heart began to thump.

'Herman?'

The doorway was empty.

My hand shook as I chose another match. This time I felt a breeze, a cold whisper across my hands. I looked behind me, telling myself it was only the wind, but my heart pumped away so loudly I thought everyone would hear.

I took a deep breath and with my back to the draught I struck the match, curling my hand around the flame. This time it hissed white, then yellow, and as the candle stub lit, it turned orange. In the shade of my hand the flame grew, flickering higher and higher until it cast my shadow round the room all bent and twisted. It began to look like a monster; it began to look like a man under a duvet.

I squeezed my eyes tight.

I saw my old house hiding behind a crackling wall of heat. Flames belched out of my bedroom window, the glass from the living room blew out into the garden and black smoke chugged from inside. I was crying and screaming at the same time, my throat hoarse, and every breath thick and laboured. Suddenly I was snatched back from the heat.

'Let go! Let go! Let go of me!'

But they wouldn't let me go.

The fire raged. I felt the wet grass tickle my bare feet and kept struggling. Thick black tendrils of smoke reached for me. Then I was yanked back again, passed from one person to another as it got colder and colder. Then there was a pair of old, wobbling arms around me, patting me and rubbing my shoulders. In the back of my mind I thought 'neighbour', then the word was gone. The lady spoke, then another person joined in, but their voices came from so far away I couldn't hear what they were saying. I was in a glass jar filled with smoke and fire and they were all on the outside. All I could hear was the spit and crackle and roar of flames, the flames that had swallowed my mum, my dad and my baby brother, but not me. A huge sob wracked my body. I wrestled myself from the old lady's embrace and lurched forwards. The flames lit me up like a spotlight on a stage. I felt the crackling heat and then . . .

. . . everything went black.

I gasped and opened my eyes, surprised to be in the French house, in the room Herman showed me. There were no fires, no smoke, and my hands still clutched the candle, shaking it, making the light leap across the walls.

I wanted to run. I wanted to run all the way back to my room and hide under the blankets, but I knew that wouldn't help. It never did. Then there was Julien. I thought of him and the fire that would end up destroying a whole side of the house, the villages and Julien himself. That's what would happen if I didn't help, if I didn't hurry, if I didn't find the medicine.

Trying to keep the candle steady, I peered round the room again, but there wasn't much more to see. There was a bookshelf on the other side of the bed with a few thin books on it, and a wooden chair in the corner next to the window. Opposite the bed was an old wardrobe and next to that a chest of drawers, both looking as though they hadn't been touched in a long time. I looked at the bedside table. The candle holder had left a clean ring in the thin film of dust that covered everything. No one had been in here for years, but the bed was neatly made and a book with a bookmark placed a quarter of the way in sat on top.

I began the quickest search ever starting with the chest

of drawers. It was empty. Then I tackled the wardrobe, but there was nothing inside except a dark-coloured suit and a pair of polished shoes. I moved on to the bookshelf, but it only held the books I'd already seen. I ignored the bed and the chair and knelt in front of the bedside cabinet with its two drawers. The top one contained a watch and some faded postcards. Underneath was a brown stained photo of a team of smiling workers squinting into the sun. Some had their arms around each other, others raised their hard hats to the sky and behind them thick tree trunks made it look like they were in a – jungle!

I turned the photo over and sure enough it said, *Team A, Congo*. This was Armuth and Herman's son's room! I turned the photo back and traced a finger over the faces, trying to see if I could tell which one he was.

Suddenly there was a thud. Then another. Someone was coming up the stairs, someone with a heavy tread, which meant it couldn't be Herman.

I looked left and right, panicking. I couldn't be found here, not after the last time, and the sewing box, and everyone thinking I'd made up seeing Herman to upset Armuth. None of them would understand, and I didn't want to upset her again. I ran to the door, shutting it carefully, thrust everything back in the drawer, then blew out the candle, placing the holder exactly where I'd found it on top of the table.

The footsteps got closer and closer. I looked round at the room. The stairs creaked and I knew they were almost on the landing. The light caught me in its prison bars stretching halfway across the bed.

Had someone heard me up here? Were they looking for me?

I needed to hide. Now!

Chapter Thirty-Three

I slipped beneath the bed and snatched my legs under as the door swung open. The moonlight shone on two swollen ankles swaying above orthopaedic shoes that squeaked as they settled.

It was Armuth.

My heart sank. I squeezed my eyes shut and hoped she couldn't see me. Upsetting her once was bad enough; I hadn't even known about Herman or her son then, but now I did – and if she found me in her son's room in the middle of the night it would look bad . . . really bad.

I clutched my knees and combed through a few excuses. Then I shook my head. They hadn't believed me even when I was telling the truth. I thought longingly of the sewing box with its reels of thread and ribbons, and felt a pang that I'd never see it again.

Armuth's shoes squeaked and my eyes shot open. But

she didn't move from the doorway.

I lay awkwardly on my side, itching to pull out a splinter that was throbbing in my little finger.

Suddenly, Armuth sniffed.

My heart raced, sure I could smell the burnt match and the candle, and that she would too. I held my breath, but with gentle squeaks her feet turned away and the door closed quietly behind her.

I held still as her footsteps creaked down the stairs, and let out a long breath. Then I gulped. I realised it was Armuth! It was her footsteps that had been following me at night. Julien said he'd never left his room so if they weren't his then Armuth was the one frightening me half to death. My cheeks burnt as I realised she must visit her son's room every night, pacing the floor and remembering him.

Now I tried the second drawer, but it wouldn't open. I rattled it, but it was stuck. I pulled harder and the whole cabinet rocked across the floor. I steadied it, cold sweat sliding down my back. I listened out for Armuth, sure I could hear her footsteps again, but no one came. I turned back to the cabinet and lifted out the top drawer to get to the one underneath and there, in the bottom, sitting there waiting, was a whole heap of medicine.

I sifted through the boxes and brown plastic bottles delicately at first, then faster and faster, frowning because the labels were all in French. Why hadn't I thought of that? Any one of them could be the right or wrong sort of medicine, and they'd be massively out of date. How was I supposed to know which was which and if they would even work? I threw them back in and gave the drawer a shove.

I thought about the photo of Armuth's son. All those smiling daces. I thought about how Julien's face had lit up when I last visited him. I thought about showing him the documents Fliss had given me and my hand went to the small of my back to check they were still there. Then I grinned. If was going to get him to read the documents – he could read the medicine labels too! I put the photo back in the drawer and closed it.

Determined now, I reached back into the second drawer and grabbed all the brown plastic bottles and the white cardboard boxes. One of them had to work. I found a crinkled paper bag hiding underneath with another box in the bottom. I piled everything into it and stood up, my knees clicking.

I pushed the chest of drawers back into place, put the candle on top and blew out the flame, making sure it was really, definitely, absolutely out. I hovered behind the door listening for footsteps, but I didn't hear anything so I grasped the handle, eased it open and ran straight into Aunt Cece.

Chapter Thirty-Four

I pulled back, but she grabbed my arm.

'What do you think you're doing?' she hissed and shook me. The bag of medicines rattled. 'And what's this?'

I stared up at her, my eyes wide, my throat so dry it felt scratched. She was in her dressing gown and slippers, but I could see some papers and a pen peeping out of one pocket. I wondered what was she doing, but before I could say anything she let go of me and grabbed the bag straight out of my hand.

'It's nothing!' I said. 'Give it back, it's mine!'

She narrowed her eyes, then in a sickly sweet voice that made my stomach turn she said, 'I know you're up to something. You remember it's up to me if you come and live with us, don't you?'

Angry tears sprung in the corner of my eyes. Rage

built in my chest like a tornado, spinning and rising until I couldn't keep it in.

'You don't care about me!' I said, wrenching my arm away from her. 'You've already decided you don't want me. Kitty told me everything.'

She stepped back as if I'd slapped her.

'And these aren't yours!' I snatched the bag. Her mouth hung open. Then, as she lunged, I pushed past her and ran towards the stairs.

'Don't you dare!'

I took the stairs two at a time, leaping up to the second floor, then racing along to the next.

'Angela! Get back here now!'

I could hear her running behind me, her heavy breaths coming hard and fast. I pulled myself up to the third floor using the bannister, ignoring a stitch poking my left side and ran down the corridor, almost skidding past the door to the mirror room. I risked a look back and saw her hand appear like a claw. At the top she turned to face me, her short hair fanned out and sticking up like a crazy cockatoo and I slipped into the room and eased the door shut.

The moon showed the mirror flush against the wall, hiding the door behind it. I ran up close, searching for the ripples, but only my reflection stared back. Nothing moved. I remembered how I'd planned to prop it open, but it was too late for that now.

I dropped the bag of medicines and pushed against the edge. Nothing. I pushed harder, digging my feet in, grinding my teeth, sweat making my hands slick. The mirror groaned and budged the tiniest bit, then stopped. I heard Aunt Cece barrelling down the corridor. She'd be at the door any second now.

'Come on,' I said.

I heaved against the sharp bevelled edge, but the mirror wouldn't move. Without thinking about how much it would hurt I stepped back then rammed my shoulder hard against it.

'I know you're in there!'

The door handle rattled. I jumped, then pushed against the mirror, digging my feet in, gritting my teeth.

The mirror groaned.

Aunt Cece swung the door wide. 'That's enough, Angela!'

I pushed harder, giving it everything I had, and with a slow, exhausted whine, the mirror finally gave way.

Flushed with triumph, I swiped up the bag, pressed the notch, pushed the door open and stepped into Julien's room.

'What are you doing? What is this? Angela, you can't hide from me.'

Her voice was a sticky oil pouring cold along my

spine. I turned to find her staring at me, hands on hips. A slow, close-lipped smile appeared as she curled one finger, beckoning me back.

'There's nowhere for you to go.'

I gulped and tightened my grip on the bag of medicines. Then I remembered the papers.

'You're the one that's up to something,' I said, reaching round to pull them out.

Her hand went to her pocket and her eyes darted to the papers I was holding out, then she took a step forwards, as if she was going to follow me into Julien's room.

'No,' I said, taking a step back, clutching the medicines and papers to my chest and, as if it had heard me, the mirror slammed shut between us.

I dropped my head and took a deep breath. The mirror had shut and I was stuck on this side. There was no going back now, even if I wanted to. I stuffed the papers back into my leggings, checked the connecting door was locked, then turned to Julien, holding up the bag of medicine.

'I did it,' I said.

But he wasn't listening and he wasn't looking.

Something was very wrong.

Chapter Thirty-Five

Julien lay sprawled across his bed, his face slick and shiny, his skin red and blistered. Candles shimmered on top of the bedside table and across the floor, making it look like he was hovering. The room tasted hot on my tongue and the smell of something putrid hit the back of my throat and made me gag.

Julien moaned.

One hand over my mouth and nose, I ran to his side. His pillows were bunched up and he slumped awkwardly against the bedstead.

'*Ange, c'est toi?*' His eyes were glassy and unfocused as his head swept left and right.

'I'm here.'

'*Ange?*'

His head lolled.

'*Mon ange?*'

'Julien?'

His eyes searched for me.

'I have medicines for you,' I said. 'Look.'

I spilt the bag onto his bed. He mumbled something, but I couldn't understand and there wasn't time to try. I swallowed a sob and rifled through the packets, emptying the cardboard boxes and turning the small brown bottles round and round, trying to make sense of the labels. I realised one contained headache pills – my old French teacher, Mrs Thomas, had said we gave her headaches all the time so I recognised that one. I threw it on the floor where it clattered and rolled under the bed.

Then I saw it – a small rectangular box hiding at the bottom of the brown paper bag. It had the two most beautiful words I had ever seen written across it: *typhoïde* and *antibiotiques*.

'Julien!'

His eyelids flickered open, but his eyes rolled back in his head.

'I've got it. I've got the right medicine!'

I tried to get him to sit up, but it was hard work. His limbs were loose and he slumped back every time I got a grip.

'*Ange?*'

'I'm here,' I said. 'Come on, sit up!'

I got both arms round him and heaved, but he slipped

back. I leant in and pulled him straight and this time he stayed upright, slumping heavily against me. His skin was boiling and he moaned.

I reached for the box, but it was difficult to open it and keep Julien from sliding back onto his damp pillows. Inside was a small brown bottle with a cap, which I snapped off. I looked for instructions, but there was nothing. I turned the bottle round and breathed a sigh of relief to find something written on it. Even though it was in French, there were numbers too.

'Three, something, something, something. Three something, something, something,' I read out loud. 'Right. Three tablets. Three times a day. Has to be.'

I repeated it again and again. Then Julien groaned and I realised it didn't matter. It was too late. He'd die without the tablets so I had to do something and I had to do it now.

I flipped the top off the bottle and spilt three of the capsules into my hand.

'Hold on.'

The jug was on the bedside table, but there was a bit of water in the glass next to it. With one hand round his back, I brought the tablets to Julien's mouth, coaxing him to take them, but spittle gathered at his lips in bubbles and he pulled his head away.

'Julien!'

I tightened one hand round the tablets and used both hands to lift him up.

'You have to take them, please. We've got plans, remember? You're going to show me the house and you're going to plant the garden and everything.'

In response, Julien's head lolled forwards and he vomited down his chest.

I leapt away. The smell was so bad I thought I might throw up too. I left him slumped while I edged off the bed. I dropped the tablets onto the bedside table and tore the soiled bed cover off him. I looked around for a sponge, some cloths, anything, but there was nothing. Flecks of vomit dribbled down his chin.

I grabbed the cleanest edge of the bed cover and dabbed it in the jug. I wiped his mouth and thought I saw a ghost of a smile.

'You've got to take the medicine, Julien,' I said. 'Now, okay?'

I threw the stinking cover on the floor and lifted him up. Syrupy vomit spread across his nightgown. He smelt sharp and rancid, but I gritted my teeth, pulled him closer and tried to breathe through my mouth to stave off the worst.

He wailed like an animal as I forced him to sit up. His eyes rolled back in his head and I knew in that moment that even if it did hurt, I had to make him take the pills.

We were pressed close, my arms wrapped round him, his head resting on my shoulder. It was sore where I'd pushed the mirror, but I ignored that and turned to the dresser. I shifted him to one arm so I could reach the tablets. All of a sudden, the door rattled. I froze. It was Julien's door, the one behind the curtain.

'*Il est là,*' Julien whispered into my hair.

His breath was stale and spoilt, but I didn't care because I'd understood what he'd said. He's here! The servant was here. But how? And why now?

'I called and called for him to come.' Julien tried to push me away, but he was as weak as a baby. 'I thought . . . what if you did not come back?'

I let him down onto the pillow and stared blankly at the door.

A key began to turn in the lock.

'*Ange?*' Julien's voice shook.

I looked at the bag. I had to get him to take the medicine. But, I remembered what he'd said, about the man telling him it would be the end of everything if anyone knew he was here.

The door began to open.

I stared at his bed, thought about slipping underneath to hide, or just giving him the medicine right now, but by then it was too late.

Chapter Thirty-Six

Julien's door swung open, snagging the velvet curtain and pushing it aside. A long black hood peered round, the rest of a cloak billowing behind it. It had wide sleeves that reached past where someone's hands would be and the whole thing fell to the floor where it pooled, giving the terrifying impression there was nothing inside it at all.

I was paralysed.

Suddenly the hood lifted and fell back to reveal tiny black eyes over a pointed grey mask covering the bottom half of a man's face. The mask was in the shape of a huge bird's beak. I shuddered. It was like something out of a nightmare circus.

The man recoiled and threw up an arm against the smell of vomit. Julien's breathing was laboured now, his skin tight, puffy and flushed a hot red. I had been frozen in place in the middle of the room, looking from one to the other, but now the man turned. He lowered his arm and gave me the full force of his angry pinprick eyes.

I glanced at Julien, but his eyes had rolled back and he couldn't help me now. I turned to my door but it was too late for that and I didn't even know if the mirror would open from this side. The man came towards me, his cloak billowing, the beaked mask turning from side to side as if it had a life of its own. I couldn't tear my eyes away. Whatever I was going to do I had to do it now.

I screamed.

The man drew back, almost tripping over his cloak. He shouted to someone over his shoulder, but his beaked mask muffled the sound. I heard a clash behind him, as if something had smashed to the floor. He turned back to me with wild eyes, making the sign of a cross. Then he threw out his arms as if he could push me away. His hood slipped back all the way.

He shouted and I cringed, rocking back and forth on my toes as if I'd decide which way to run any second, except there was nowhere for me to go.

He reached the bottom of Julien's bed and blanched as the foul smell hit him again. I waited for him to shout again, but he didn't. Instead, he rested his hands on the cot rails. They were shaking. His chest was heaving. Slowly he lowered his beaked mask to reveal brown hair, deep grooves etched into his forehead, sideburns that were turning grey and a full mouth twisted in horror.

'*Vous êtes un fantôme,*' he growled.

I frowned, trying to translate, trying to remember every French lesson I could. *Fantôme*. It sounded like phantom. Did he mean ghost?

'*Partez!*'

He threw out his arm again and it was clear he wanted me gone. I looked at my doorway, then back at Julien. He whimpered, then fell silent. His head flopped at an awkward angle. I felt a pull in my stomach. He needed medicine and he needed it now, but the man slipped between me and Julien's bed, like he was protecting him from me. His head whipped towards the door he'd come through. I remembered Julien telling me that no one could know he was there. Then he looked over his shoulder at me and I got it. *Fantôme* did mean ghost! He was scared.

'*Pars d'ici!*' he said.

I was sure that meant get out or go away, or something like that, but I couldn't move.

The man reached to touch Julien's head, and jerked his hand back as if he'd been burnt.

Julien whimpered. I stepped closer, but the man glared. This time I glared right back, hiding my shaking hands behind me. Julien was mumbling rubbish while the man and I had a stare-off, and I tried not to run and hide. Suddenly Julien managed to speak.

'*Oncle Nicolas.*'

The man dropped his head.

Nicolas Brodeur! I remembered the newspaper picture Fliss found in the library book. He'd had much more of a beard in it, but it was definitely him. The only one who survived the fire.

Julien groaned. He was trying to sit up, but kept slipping back down. My top half leant forward to help, but my feet felt glued to the floorboards, and even that small movement brought a poisonous stare from the man. I gulped.

Julien looked at me before speaking to his uncle in English.

'Why are you keeping me here?' he asked. 'Why have you forgotten me?'

But before his uncle could answer, Julien yelled, 'Where is my mother? Where is Philippe?'

His uncle blanched. Then he let go of the cot bars, walked over and shut the door firmly. He stood with his back to us, his shoulders heaving. I slipped to Julien's side and when his uncle turned round I stared back, my eyes wide. I gulped again and again. He shook his head and closed his eyes. I hoisted Julien up, wrapping one arm round him to keep him steady. He reached for my other hand and squeezed it. I squeezed back.

All of a sudden his uncle lunged. Julien flinched, but

his uncle was only getting to his knees. He began to unlace his mask, muttering, '*Je suis désolé, je suis désolé.*'

I knew that meant sorry.

His uncle let the mask drop to the floor and shook his head. His brown curls fell into his eyes.

'In English,' Julien said.

His uncle looked at me then spoke.

'I have been remiss,' he said. I choked.

'You speak English too,' I said.

He stared at me, his brows meeting in the middle, then his gaze dropped to my hand in Julien's and he frowned. He shook his head, shrugged his shoulders and without looking at me directly, answered, 'Some.'

Julien coughed. His chest rattled like it was filled with marbles and he couldn't seem to catch his breath. I reached round for the tablets then realised Julien's uncle was talking to me.

'I was too frightened to tell him,' he said. Dread rolled off him. 'I didn't want to make him worse.'

Julien groaned and my hand itched to grab the pills, but I thought his uncle might stop me.

'I did what I thought was right for him, for me, for all of us.' His uncle nodded then looked up at me. 'I sent everyone away, even the servants. Only I know he is here. I have been looking after him.' He rubbed his forehead with his hands. 'But it no longer matters. Because if you are here then it is already the end.' His voice broke. 'The end of everything.' He flicked a glance at Julien then looked straight at me. 'I will tell you what happened.'

Chapter Thirty-Seven

Nicolas brought one hand to his heart. 'His mother, my sister, she died. She was dead when we opened the carriage.' He let his hand drop. 'His stepfather was already sick.' He paused. 'Philippe died a few days later.'

His nose turned up when he said 'Philippe' so I could tell he hadn't liked the stepfather very much.

'No! It is not true,' Julien said, lifting his head for a moment, but it dropped forward onto his chin. I felt Julien's pain. It plucked at things I kept buried deep inside. I took his hand in mine and squeezed it, but his muscles had gone limp. So much heat radiated from his body, it was almost unbearable to be touching him. With the shimmering haze of the candles and the smell of vomit, I started to feel dizzy. I looked longingly at the tablets, then back at Nicolas.

His uncle shook his head and I noticed lines either side

of his mouth as if he laughed a lot once. Now they made him look sad. As he knelt closer, his voice softened. 'They died, Julien, and the man who drove the carriage died, and two of my servants who cared for your stepfather in the house died.'

He stood up and ran his hands through his hair. 'The priest who blessed your mother. He also died.' He slammed a fist against the side of the bed. 'They brought the disease with them!'

'Typhoid,' I whispered.

Julien's uncle stared at me. His mouth twisted, his eyes closed for a second. 'We were isolated for two months.' He looked at his nephew. 'I had to hide you. Everyone thought you were dead.' He paused. 'It was safer to let them think this,' he added, looking at me. 'If anyone knew he was here the people of the village would burn down this house and everything and everyone in it.'

Julien groaned and tried to lift his head. I shook mine in disbelief.

'It is happening all around us. The people are scared and the magistrate, the judge of our region, has a lot to lose.' He looked at Julien. 'I am trying to keep you alive.'

His hand reached towards his nephew, but Julien shrank into me.

'You locked me away.' Spittle flew from his lips. 'You're waiting for me to die so you can inherit the house.'

Julien coughed. Bubbles of spit formed around his mouth. They began to froth. I turned to reach for the medicines on the table, but Julien pulled me back, squeezing my hand. His uncle's eyes fixed on that. He shook his head.

'We have been lucky, Julien,' he said, 'so lucky. Many towns and villages have suffered greatly.' He stood and grabbed the cot rails. 'Families lost. Estates ruined. Houses destroyed.' He let that sink in then turned to me. 'I am hiding him, yes.'

We squeezed our hands tight.

'But I am trying to help him.' He faced Julien. 'I have kept watch on you. I have kept you fed.' He sucked in a breath. 'I even kept the truth about your mother and Philippe from you to save you more pain.' He threw up his hands. 'I had no choice! I am trying to keep the house in the family.' He picked up his mask and fiddled with it. 'I have a responsibility to the estate. I have tenants to support. I have been trying to help you, not frighten you, boy. You must understand.'

But Julien didn't answer. He could barely keep his eyes open. I tried to shift him, but he seemed somehow heavier.

'I have tried to nurse you as best I could, but nothing has worked. I tried some of the best doctors, those I could trust to keep the secret. I put medicine in your food. One even suggested this mask to protect me.'

I stared at the beak mask.

He shook his head. 'I am sorry, Julien.'

Julien's head lolled left then right and his words became a mixture of English and French that didn't make any sense. I couldn't wait any longer.

'Help me. Now!' I yelled at his uncle.

Julien's uncle shook his head at me. 'I have tried everything.'

'I have medicine that will help him,' I said, 'at least I think it will. I mean, we should try it, but you need to help me lift him.'

Suddenly there was a knock at the curtained door.

I pulled my arm away and Julien fell back against the pillows with an agonising groan.

With a look at me, Julien's uncle turned to the door and pressed himself against it. I heard a muffled voice before he slumped, his head drooping. He nodded to himself, said a few words back I didn't understand, then turned to me.

'That was my man. We are lost. It is the end.' He came back to Julien's bedside and put his head in his hands.

'But I have medicine,' I said. 'I can help.'

He shook his head. 'The magistrate is coming. Someone has betrayed us. A servant must have talked. They want to see the boy. The villagers . . . they know, and are afraid.'

He looked behind me at the barred window.

'It's not too late,' I said. 'It can't be!' I grabbed the tablets and the glass of water. 'Hold him up, support his head.'

His uncle didn't move. Then with a look at his mask he threw it aside and wedged himself against Julien and held his head up. I leant across and tried to pop the tablets in Julien's mouth, but he kept shaking his head.

'No!'

I think he thought I was someone else, someone trying to hurt him, but there was no time to explain.

'Keep him still,' I said and his uncle wrapped his hands round Julien's head. It looked as if he was strangling him or was about to rip his head off, but I concentrated on getting the tablets down Julien's throat.

Suddenly Julien's body went rigid. A strange red rash was crawling from beneath his collar. I'd never seen anything like it, but I remembered Julien describing the rash his mother had right before she died.

'Hurry!' his uncle said.

I shoved the tablets into Julien's mouth and his uncle forced his head back. I poured water on top of them and his uncle clamped one hand over his mouth. Julien's body jerked, then his arms and legs thrashed out. The glass of water went flying, smashing against the floor and shattering into tiny pieces. I reached for Julien's arms and held them. Slowly Julien's seizure stopped. His breathing tapered to a shallow wheeze. He looked almost peaceful. If I hadn't known better I'd have said he was sleeping. I parted his lips. The tablets were gone; he'd swallowed them. I combed his damp hair off his face with my fingers. I looked up to see his uncle watching me.

'Who are you?'

I sat back, looked at Julien and sighed. 'I'm his friend,' I said.

We watched Julien's chest rise and fall in silence.

Nicolas cleared his throat. 'And what do we do now?'

'Now,' I said, 'we wait.'

I looked round the room at all the mess. Most of the candles were down to their stubs if not burnt out completely. Time passed slowly. I couldn't sleep. I kept worrying about whether the tablets would work and watching Julien for any sign that they were. Even if they did, would it be enough for the magistrate?

I heard a faint bell, *ting-ting-ting-ting*ing. I counted twelve. Midnight. It was August twenty-eighth, the day Julien was supposed to die.

I looked up. The room was dark, but from the barred window, a strange orange light was glowing, throwing eerie shapes around the room.

'What's that?' I asked.

Julien's uncle looked at me with pity. 'That,' he said, 'is the villagers. They are coming in case the magistrate is right.'

Chapter Thirty-Eight

'No,' I said, shaking my head, 'the medicine will work. We just have to wait. We can make them wait.'

So we waited and we waited, the orange light inching so close I could hear it crackle and spit, though I knew that was impossible. I thought about what Julien had said, about villages and houses burnt to the ground. I thought about the newspaper article saying a whole side of the house had gone. Would the medicines make any difference? Would we all die anyway? I was trapped here too. I looked at his uncle. He stared back.

Neither of us spoke.

Orange light began to creep through the gaps in the wooden boards nailed across the window until it filled the room. Then we heard a noise.

Julien's uncle ran round the bed and prised the corner off one of the boards, pulling it back so he could see outside.

'Is it them?' I said, my voice high. 'Are they here?'

He thrust out a hand so I'd be quiet, his head shifting left and right as he tried to take in as much as he could through the gap. Then he turned to me, his face grave.

'The villagers are at the gate.'

I gasped, my hand to my mouth.

He held up his hands as if to calm me. 'I could not see the magistrate. I think they are waiting for him.'

I shook my head as he made for the door. 'Wait!'

He turned back. 'There is no time. They should wait for the magistrate, but I fear they will not. I must face them. I must stop them, tell them Julien is well. I have to do something.'

'No, wait!'

I'd been running everything over and over in my head. Before, I'd thought Julien had died of typhoid.

I looked at him. Watched his chest rise and fall.

But then Fliss had translated the books for me. Now the villagers were here to burn down the house. I thought of the face at the window, the flames behind it. Were they a warning about the house burning down? In the end, was that how he died?

I squeezed my eyes shut. I heard the roar and felt the crackle, snap and whump of yellow, orange and red flames.

'No!' I forced my eyes open.

Julien's uncle was staring out of the door. I could see a large window reaching from the floor to the ceiling behind him. It was filled with flickering orange flames. We were surrounded.

'I can stop them,' I said.

His uncle turned to me.

I took a deep breath. 'I can save the us.'

Chapter Thirty-Nine

His uncle's eyes fixed on mine.

'I mean it. I can save us and the house.'

We both looked at Julien, watched his shallow breathing in the crackling orange light.

'I can talk to them,' I said. 'Show them I'm not sick.'

Julien's uncle shook his head. 'It's the boy they want to see.'

I ran to Julien's side and grabbed the sleeve of his nightshirt.

'But do they need to see him up close?'

I was hoping we could hold off the villagers to give the magistrate enough time to get here. I looked at Julien. And enough time for the tablets to work.

Nicolas narrowed his eyes, understanding me, then he ran over and helped me take Julien's nightshirt off. Without it, Julien began to shiver and I pulled the covers up under his chin, covering his skinny frame. I shrugged my cardigan and shoes off and slipped the nightshirt over my head. It felt heavy, damp with sweat, and smelt so bad I thought I might be sick.

Julien's uncle gestured at my hair and I pulled my hairband out and let it fall across my face. It wasn't exactly the same colour as Julien's, and it was much longer, but it would do. Nicolas beckoned to me and I followed him out of the room.

Outside the attic, the walls curved round. I was at the top of a tower. Below me a staircase of stone led down into darkness, and straight across from Julien's room was the tall window. Julien's uncle unlocked it and pushed it open. The glass doors slammed back against the walls as if pulled by the wind. I felt as if the stone beneath my feet was vibrating. Then I heard it.

The roar.

Julien's uncle held out his hand.

I took a deep breath. I could feel the vibrations in my teeth now. My whole body was shaking. But it was now or never. I stepped forward.

Below us a mob surged around the house like it was one giant yellow-orange monster. I squeezed my eyes shut and thought of my dad under the duvet trying to save me. Now I was trying to save Julien. I had to do this. I forced my eyes open.

Julien's uncle was shouting in French, but I didn't think anyone was listening. The crowd wove left and right. The flame shapes made me dizzy and sick and remember more things I didn't want to.

Then Julien's uncle grabbed my arm and held it up.

The crowd shushed.

He pulled me forward and someone in the crowd yelled, then another, then another.

Julien's uncle shouted back to the mob, shaking my arm every time he took a breath. I stared at the sea of people below and felt my eyes swim. My legs buckled.

Julien's uncle turned and glared at me. I steadied myself.

The crowd below was getting restless. They surged towards the house again. I felt a wall of heat and I could taste smoke in the back of my throat. I swallowed. It wasn't working.

'Tell me what to say!'

Julien's uncle let go of my hand.

'Wait! I can do it,' I said. 'Just tell me what to say!'

He shook his head. 'It's too late,' he said, staring at the mob below. 'They are out of control. They won't listen.'

I shook my head, grabbed his hand with both of mine. 'No, we have to try,' I said, my heart beating triple time. I took a breath. 'You say it in French and I'll copy you. They'll think I'm Julien and they'll listen.'

Smoke twisted its way up towards us. I bent over coughing, then straightened up. 'Won't they?'

Julien's uncle shouted some words at me, but the hiss and spit and crackle and roar of the crowd and the flames drowned them.

'Again!' I yelled at him.

'*Je vais bien.*'

I knew that meant all is good or I am fine or something. I yelled it out.

But the crowd pushed forward. No one could hear me.

The smoke reached us. I coughed and reared back. It was close, too close. I couldn't stay here any longer. I turned to run back into the room then stopped. Julien lay in his bed. The only way to save him, to save all of us, was to do this. I squeezed my eyes shut, took three deep breaths, then I turned back to his uncle and faced the crowd. Nicolas took my hand in his.

Together we shouted a third time.

'*Je vais bien!*'

There was a shout from below. Then another. Julien's uncle shouted back, but that's when I heard glass breaking. Then there was screaming. Then I was screaming. A wall of flame rushed up the walls towards us. Then everything went black.

Chapter Forty

Silence. Then, I heard someone laugh. A sparkling, tinkling sound with a melody – and that was completely weird because it was coming from me.

I was running, but it was hard to run because something kept getting in my way and tangling my feet. I looked down and found them hidden under voluminous skirts in a fabric that looked like a thick embroidered curtain. I traced the pattern of green swirls and a deep, rich purple thread in tiny linked circles that made flower shapes. I picked out the petals with my fingertips. It was beautiful, but it was also really hot. I tried to lift the skirts and free my feet, but they were super heavy and besides, something was holding me back and stopping me from being able to bend. I felt my ribs. I was wearing some kind of bodice and it was tight, so tight it was hard to breathe, and I had to take tiny, shallow breaths. I traced the delicate lace that lay across my chest.

'*Prêt ou pas, j'arrive!*'

Ready or not, I'm coming!

I whipped my head round and spied a boy facing away from me. He leant against one of the thick trees surrounding us, his head tucked into his arm. He began to turn and I caught my breath. It was Julien – except he looked so different.

He wasn't the skinny, sick boy I knew. He was taller and he'd filled out. He stood with one foot resting nonchalantly against the trunk, his blond hair lighter and flopping foppishly into his eyes. I drank him in. He looked so fit and healthy, nothing like the boy in the attic, but at the same time, it was definitely him. The dappled light through the leaves caught his eyes and made them sparkle. He saw me staring and laughed.

'*Tu dois courir!*'

I grinned. Then, as he took a step towards me I picked up my skirts and did what he'd said I should do. I ran.

Within a split second he was chasing me and I squealed, laughing and shaking my head because it was so hard to run. The dress dragged against the tall grass as I tried to weave in and out of the trees. I could hear him getting closer and tried to run faster, dipping between patches of sun-dappled light and colder shade as the trees began to thin out. Then he grabbed hold of my hand and pulled me back. I slipped, giggling as I turned to stare into his bright eyes. The sunlight had caught him in a spotlight, turning his blond hair to white. As I slid to the ground he fell with me and together we tumbled into the grass. My skirts tangled with my legs and my giggling became uncontrollable. Julien smiled and leant in close, so close our lips were almost touching. I watched his lips part and say my name over and over. Then I closed my eyes and he kissed me.

'*Ange?*'

There was coughing, croaking, the sound of a throat clearing phlegm. I heard him say my name. I smiled. The sun was shining. The air smelt sweet.

'Angela?'

I bolted upright, looking left and right. There was a flattened shape in the bedspread where I'd been slumped across Julien's bed. It had been changed to one with a red leaf pattern and smelt fresh. I blinked. His uncle had gone, but Julien was awake. I shook myself. Julien was awake and alive!

I stared at him. He tugged at his fringe where it flopped into his eyes and I noticed it had been washed. His skin was pink, not red, and the puffiness had gone. He looked tired and drawn, but there was a light in his eyes. I could see that the fever had gone.

'We didn't want to wake you,' he said. 'Can you help me to sit?'

I leant towards him, then something stopped me. It wasn't just the dream, though I could still feel the brush of his lips against mine. My cheeks felt warm and I tried to cover up my blush by helping him without actually touching, which was impossible.

He caught my hand and squeezed it. The dream suddenly felt as close as if it was just another door off his room.

'Medicine!' I said, dropping his hand and reaching for the box, which had been placed neatly on the dresser, along with a fresh pitcher of water and a new glass.

'You should take the rest of them. Three tablets, three times a day.' I shrugged. 'Was I right?'

He nodded.

I busied myself topping up a glass of water that was already three-quarters full and waited for him to take his pills. He tilted his head and watched me. When he reached for my hand again, I spoke before he could take it.

'Where's your uncle?'

'Angela.'

'Is everything all right with him? And what about the villagers? And the house?'

I turned to the door, which was shut, then to the window, but only a pale dawn light peeked through.

There was no smell of smoke, nothing looked burnt. I looked down, but Julien's nightshirt was gone. I was wearing my own clothes.

Julien raised his eyebrows and smiled. 'It is more than all right. You saved us.'

I shook my head trying to remember what had happened. I'd gone out onto the balcony. I remembered the mob surging. I remembered shouting out and no one listening. I remembered breaking glass and . . .

I felt myself sway.

'They listened,' Julien said. 'They listened to you.'

I looked at him.

He smiled. 'The servants came back and helped us. They pushed the crowd back. They heard you. They thought you were me. It gave us enough time for the magistrate to arrive. He came in and talked to my uncle and then to me.' He gestured to the room. 'Uncle Nicolas did all this.'

I noticed the whole place had been cleared. All the old candles had been taken away and a large burgundy-coloured rug lay across most of the floor. The curtains across his door and the window had been taken down. My bag of medicine had been folded over and sat on the bedside table. Something about that nagged at me like an itch.

'The doctors told him to lock me away like a monk

in a cell, to purge the sickness, and to have no one but a trusted servant bring me food and water.'

He looked around at the transformed room. 'They told him to keep away, but he was here all along. He *was* the servant! He didn't leave me.' He smiled. 'He has gone to get a new doctor so they can confirm I am alive – alive and safe and not contagious.'

He watched me closely. 'He says Doctor Chantemesse of Paris is an expert, although the cold baths he recommends do not sound enticing at all.' He grinned. 'He called me, "my boy".'

Julien shrugged his shoulders, as if that was silly and childish, but he couldn't hide his happiness.

'Nicolas has sent someone for the notary, to sign for the house, for my inheritance, but the doctor first. Just as a precaution.'

He shook his head. 'The villagers set the gatehouse and some of outbuildings alight, but the fire was stopped in time, thanks to the servants. They organised the carts to carry water from the river and put everyone to work.' He sighed. 'The magistrate believed I was well. Just a fever, we told him.' He closed his eyes, then opened them and smiled. 'The house is saved, Angela.'

Julien paused, watching me. 'Angela?'

I was listening, but I was also staring at the paper bag full of medicines. Then I realised what was bugging me.

It was the pills. The doctor couldn't find out about the pills. Nobody could know about them. I didn't know when antibiotics were invented, but I was pretty sure it wasn't 1898. I felt light-headed. That sort of thing could change history. I gulped. Like saving someone who was supposed to die.

'Angela?'

Julien leant his head towards me and smiled. 'Nicolas said to give you a thousand thanks.'

I looked at him, smiling and so happy. I gave back a small smile of my own. I wouldn't change what I'd done even if I could, but there was only so much that seemed right to change.

'You can't tell them,' I said, grabbing his arms. 'You can't tell anyone!'

Chapter Forty-One

Julien frowned.

'I mean the medicines,' I told him. 'You can't tell anyone about them.'

He stared at me for a moment then nodded.

'Because, well, the medicines aren't supposed to be . . .'

I picked up the small brown bottle, but my eyes were drawn to a selection of gilt framed pictures behind it. There was one of a beautiful young blond woman with perfectly curled hair and another of her with a dashing older man in some sort of uniform. Next to that was one of her with a taller man with the same curls, only darker and with bushy brown sideburns, no lines on his forehead or grey hairs. It was Julien's Uncle Nicolas. He looked young and happy. They both did.

'He brought them for me,' Julien said, pointing to a small picture locket. There was a pinkish rose painted on the outside, and inside a picture on the left of a young girl and on the right, a young boy.

'My mother and Oncle Nicolas,' Julien said, but he didn't have to; I could see the family resemblance. I touched the edge of the locket thinking how amazing it would've been if I could have saved his mum too, if I could have saved all of them.

I shook myself and picked up the bag of pills. 'You can't tell the doctor about my medicine, Julien.' I chewed my lip, staring at the bag. 'Because it's a secret.'

He smiled. 'Like you?' he said, cocking his head to the side. '*Est elle un fantôme?* That's what my uncle asked.'

He reached for me again. I put the bag of pills aside and let him take my hand. 'I told him maybe you were a ghost.' He smiled, his eyes crinkling before he looked at the bag in my hand. 'They do not matter. I will inherit now and the house is saved. I will show my face and walk in the village soon and they will all know I am well. I can finally begin work on my plans, mine and Philippe's plans, for the grounds. I will plant more walnut trees – a grove of walnut trees! It will work, I know it, and the estate will be prosperous again.' He grinned. 'And there will be new books. My uncle says our history begins today. A new age.'

He pulled me closer, shaking his head very gently. 'And I will keep your secret, *fantôme.*'

I closed my eyes and thought about my dream. It wasn't just the kiss, though that was totally amazing, it was much more. I wanted the warm feeling of the sun on my face and running so fast it made me laugh. I wanted to stay in that place.

I opened my eyes and Julien's face was right there in front of mine. Neither of us spoke. I was thinking a hundred thoughts at a thousand miles per hour. I was thinking if I could stay here instead, with him. I was thinking about Aunt Cece's face, as the mirror slammed shut between us, and how there was nothing left for me back there. Then I was thinking that it felt like I knew Julien, even though it hadn't been for very long. But then I thought how he didn't know the real me, how he didn't know what I'd done. I shivered. He wouldn't want me to stay if he knew.

I broke off and looked over at the window. Light was creeping through the broken boards and across the room like thin, spindly fingers. I could feel his eyes on me as I walked over and ripped the rotting boards off one by one till sunrise flooded the attic. It was morning.

Today was the day I was due to go home, whatever that meant. Aunt Cece would drop me back at the home and leave me there. I knew Kitty was right. Aunt Cece didn't want me, and I'd only made it worse running off with her papers. I'd be moved on to another kids' home and then another one. I'd already been in three.

The sun shone on my face but I felt cold through and through. Then Julien spoke.

'I am better,' he said quietly, 'but you do not seem to be happy about that.'

I turned to him, a prickling behind my eyes. 'I am,' I said. 'Really, I'm so happy for you.'

He raised his eyebrows and shrugged. 'But you like me better sick?'

'No!' I said.

He laughed then and it was the laugh of the boy in my dream, the one who'd chased me, pulled me to the ground, then kissed me. I wanted that so much it tugged at my chest and made my cheeks burn. I looked away.

'No,' I said, 'it's just that it's tomorrow already.'

I looked back at the sun rising pink and orange and warm. If I was going to say something about staying, it would have to be now. I took a deep breath, but nothing came out. The words were stuck in my throat.

'It is my birthday,' Julien said.

I nodded and swallowed. 'Look. It's my last day here,' I said in a rush. 'I'm supposed to leave today, for England.'

I let the words hang in the air between us. They felt like solid things. I couldn't know what he was thinking, but his eyes didn't leave mine. I could feel the prickling at the corners of my eyes turn into tears, but I didn't look away.

'I don't want to go back,' I whispered.

I couldn't say any more. Whatever it was in my throat seemed to have grown so big it stopped me speaking.

'You don't want to go back to England? With your family?'

I shook my head, then shrugged. I wanted to explain, to tell him about my dream and that I wanted to stay here with him in 1898, but I couldn't say it. I'd lied to him about my parents and not just once. In my head I heard Aunt Cece, Mrs Morrison, Kitty and Fliss telling me off for making up stories, and that other voice, the one I heard all the time, the one telling me he wouldn't want me to stay once he knew me, once he knew what I'd done. That was the loudest. I shook my head.

'It doesn't matter.'

'But your parents –'

'I said it doesn't matter.'

Julien beckoned me over and I sat on his left side, not quite on, not quite off the bed, one leg on the floor. I tried to shake the voice off, but I couldn't; it filled my head. Like the kids in the home, it chanted, 'Liar, liar, liar, liar,' when I said my dad was coming to get me. Liar, liar. Like that was all I was.

'Angela, tell me what you are thinking.'

I shook my head. My leg swung against the cot rails and I picked at a nail.

'Angela?'

My mind began to whirr. I looked at my hands. 'My parents won't want me back,' I started then stopped. 'I mean, they prefer my brother and they never wanted a daughter, so –' I stopped again. 'In fact, they have too many kids. There's seven of us so they won't really miss me or anything.'

I took a breath, then started again, but Julien covered my hand with his and for a second I stopped thinking, stopped fidgeting. His hand felt warm, but he wasn't burning hot. He really was better. I looked up and he smiled, and his eyes were the same clear, sparkling eyes as the Julien in my dream.

'Tell me the truth,' he said gently.

I took a deep breath.

Chapter Forty-Two

I shook my head. 'There's nothing for me to go back to,' I said in a small voice.

I looked away. He kept hold of my hand while I concentrated on the window: the bits of wood hanging limp where I'd broken the rotted slats off, a nail sticking out at a dangerous angle, the sun lighting a path towards me.

It was so much easier to think up a lie or a story, to want the things I said to be true, but Julien kept me tethered to his side and I stopped thinking, stopped trying to come up with something that wasn't the truth. I stopped thinking about what would happen if I told him everything, what he would think of me. I sat in the sun, letting his stillness wash over me. After a while, I realised I was speaking.

'There was a fire.'

He waited as I traced the pattern of his quilt with my fingernail.

'My parents died.' My voice hitched, my finger paused. 'My baby brother died.' My hands balled into fists and I mouthed the next words. 'It was all my fault.'

A huge sob escaped my throat. I tried to choke it back down, but I couldn't. Bottled up tears spilt over my cheeks and dripped onto the blankets. I wiped them with my sleeve, but they kept coming. Julien was silent, but I realised he was stroking my hand. Something started to loosen inside me as I said the words out loud for the first time.

'I couldn't save them,' I said. 'My dad saved me, but he went back for my mum and my brother.' Words tumbled out. 'My mum was in Ben's room, at the back of the house. She was sleeping there because he'd been sick and he'd kept me up – he'd kept all of us up. He was so noisy. He screamed all the time. I'd complained because I had school and homework and I couldn't sleep, I couldn't think. So Mum slept in Ben's room with him, at the back of the house. My dad came and got me out. Then he went back for them.' I tried to swallow the lump in my throat, but it wouldn't go down. 'I never saw any of them again.'

Julien pulled me and I fell against him. My ribs heaved as I wept into his side, my snuffling sounding so much like Armuth's it made me cry even harder. I thought about poor Herman and how she'd lost her son as well as her husband. Armuth and I were the same. We'd lost everyone. I imagined myself like her, found years later by someone wondering what the scary noise was, though I didn't have any photo albums left to cry over. They'd all been destroyed in the fire. I sobbed.

Julien tightened his arms around me. My head nestled into his neck. I could smell the salty tang of his sweat and the fresh shirt he was wearing. He smelt like dappled sunlight and warm, end of summer days. He held me until my sobs began to subside.

'It wasn't your fault,' he said gently.

'I couldn't save them,' I whispered into his chest. 'I tried, but people held me back.'

'It wasn't your fault,' he whispered.

I sat up.

'It wasn't your fault,' he said again, holding my gaze.

'But it was!' I said, pulling away. 'Didn't you hear what I just said?'

'But it wasn't your fault, *ange*, just like it wasn't my uncle's fault that my mother and Philippe died.'

I tried to speak, but he put his palm against my cheek. 'How could it have been your fault?'

'I was angry,' I said. 'I complained about Ben all the time.' I paused, looking at my hands. 'And I lied. I said

I had to study for a test, but really I just wanted some peace and quiet.' My chest heaved as I sobbed. 'I told them I wished I was an only child. I didn't mean it!'

I tried to pull away, but Julien wouldn't let me this time.

'So it *was* my fault!' I said. 'It *was* my fault my mum was with Ben and my dad had to go back and get them and if I hadn't said anything, if I'd just been nicer and not lied, if I'd just not . . .'

Julien shook his head. 'All this time you've thought something that wasn't true.'

He stroked my tangled hair. 'Like I did, thinking my uncle had abandoned me,' he said, 'and it has caused you so much pain.' A lone curl fell onto my face. 'The fire was not your fault,' he said gently, and tucked the stray curl behind my ear.

I tried to look away.

'Say it.'

I pretended not to hear.

Julien took both my hands in his. 'Look at me.'

I shook my head.

'Angela, say it.'

I looked up and quietly, so quietly that only he could hear, I whispered, 'It wasn't my fault?'

He nodded.

'It wasn't my fault,' I said again.

I breathed out then, a breath like a wave I felt through my whole body. It took the lump in my throat with it. I felt emptied and a little dizzy and light-headed. My stomach growled. I couldn't remember how long it had been since I last ate. It must have been yesterday morning.

Morning!

Armuth was probably up and Aunt Cece wouldn't be far behind, if she wasn't standing in front of the mirror waiting for me, that was. She and Uncle Vaughn and Kitty and Fliss would be packed and ready to leave after breakfast. They'd drop me off, Aunt Cece would tell Mrs Morrison I'd been awful, and that would be that. None of them wanted me around. None of them would miss me, not really. Julien and I had both lost our families. I looked at our clasped hands. I'd told him everything. He knew I'd made up stories and he was still holding my hand. If I was going to stay in 1898, I had to ask him now. I took a deep breath then looked into his eyes.

Chapter Forty-Three

But it was Julien who spoke first.

'And you do have something to go back to.'

I frowned.

He reached over me and for a split second I thought he might kiss me. I felt my cheeks get hot, but instead he lifted a sheaf of papers from the bedside table. They'd been folded and tucked behind the photo frames. My papers! The papers I'd hidden down my leggings. A hand went to my back.

'They fell out when they took off the old nightshirt,' he said.

I waited for more. He shook his fringe off his face and leant forward.

'You do have something to go back to,' he said. Then he smiled, his eyes crinkling. 'Your parents left you a home.' He smoothed out the papers and pointed to my dad's name. 'See here? This is a legal agreement. Your father is the current owner of Maison de Noyer, with his half-sister.'

If I looked confused, it was because I was totally confused.

'My dad didn't have a half-sister. He was an only child.'

He touched my arm. 'Her name is Armuth Brodeur.'

'What?'

I grabbed the papers. I hadn't noticed her name before, but it was there, two pages over in really tiny writing. I shook my head. It was true. Armuth was my dad's half-sister and she was a Brodeur!

'You know this woman?' he asked.

I nodded.

'But you did not know about the house,' he said.

I shook my head in disbelief.

'Then how did you get these papers?'

'My cousin, Fliss,' I said. 'She said I should see them.' My words slowed. 'She got them from my aunt's handbag.' I looked at Julien. 'Why didn't my aunt say anything?'

Julien looked at the papers and shifted awkwardly.

'Tell me if you know!'

He pointed to the third page. 'This part here,' he said. 'An addendum.'

I shrugged.

'It means something new has been added to the original document.'

I nodded, but I still couldn't read the French.

'In the event of your father's death, the house would pass to your mother and in the event of her death . . .'

He stopped.

'Go on,' I whispered.

'In the event of her death, it passes to you and your brother.' He looked up. 'But if you're not of age, he offers the choice of two guardians, his half-sister or a Mrs C Williams.'

A hot shard of anger ran through me.

'Aunt Cece,' I said.

'But is she not also related to this woman?'

I shook my head.

'She's my mum's sister, but my mum hardly ever mentioned her. They weren't close.'

Julien looked back at the papers. 'You are to live under their care.' Then he frowned. 'The addendum says though that this Mrs C Williams will buy the whole house. There is an application made for your half and a deed of sale drawn up.'

I shook my head. 'I don't understand.'

Julien gripped the papers. 'It means she will own the whole house. She is supposed to manage your half for you until you are of age, and longer if you're not deemed responsible, but . . .'

'What?'

Julien studied the papers. 'You are supposed to live under her care, unless she can prove there is a reason why this would not be suitable.' He looked up. 'She has written that there is.'

I ground my teeth. 'I can't believe she would do this. I mean, she's always going on about me being more responsible, but I've got no one, nothing. I lost everything!' I shook my head. 'And she's supposed to take care of me, but she'll just go back to Mrs Morrison and say I upset everyone and they'll let her have the whole house? Just like that?'

Julien opened his mouth to say something, but I ignored him and marched over to the door and back again.

'And Armuth said the house was failing. I mean, I could have helped her, couldn't I, if I own half of it? But instead she's selling it to my aunt.'

I stopped and slapped a hand to my forehead. 'That's what Aunt Cece meant when she said it was a goldmine and that's why she was offering Armuth more money!'

I started pacing again, shaking my head. 'I heard her talking,' I explained to Julien. 'So this means she's buying the whole house and getting it cheap because it's falling apart and then what? She'll do it up and sell it to someone else for tons more, keeping all the money for herself and my cousins, and all the while I wouldn't know a thing! How could she do this?'

Julien tried to catch my eye. 'Angela?'

'They should have told me! Both of them.'

'Angela?'

'I can't believe Aunt Cece would be so evil.'

'Angela!'

'What?' I stopped pacing and threw myself on his bed.

'Stay,' he said, squeezing my hand. 'Leave them to their scheming and stay here with me.'

I blinked and blinked and blinked some more.

'Really? I mean, really?' I said, sitting up. 'Because I would love that.'

I leant back against the cot rails and gazed idly at the pictures on the top of the table. My eyes fell on the bag of medicine. Something still niggled me about it, as I listened to Julien gabble about the house and the grounds.

'Philippe wanted to plant more walnut trees because the soil is perfect. He had so many ideas, you would not believe. We discussed it often. How we would plant and where and why some soil was better than others. He said walnut trees had a special quality. He felt they were the future. A future you can be part of.'

I could feel the sun on my face and heavy skirts swishing round my legs as I imagined walking through the orchard with him.

'And you will still be in the house. I will own Maison

de Noyer now and we will look after it together!'

Everything Julien said made a sort of sense, but my chest felt tight and it was nothing to do with a bodice.

I sat up and grabbed his hand. 'Wait.'

'For the house, it would have been my mother who made the decisions. She had excellent taste. But you could make it to your taste.'

'Julien, listen!'

He frowned and I shook my head.

'I can't stay,' I said. 'I want to, I really do, but I can't. It's not right.' I looked again at the bag of medicine.

'But you said you would love to.'

I nodded my head, gulping back tears. It was true, but the medicines . . . They'd been niggling me and then there was Armuth's last name – Brodeur. She must be descended from Uncle Nicolas. What if I stayed and that changed everything so much that she was never born and my dad was never born and . . . Oh, it was so complicated. I shook my head then took a breath. The medicines weren't supposed to be here and, no matter how much I wanted it, neither was I.

He pulled me to him. 'Stay, Angela, please.'

His lips were right next to mine. All I could think about was the kiss in my dream. I leant closer. I could be so happy here, but I thought of Armuth, of my mum and dad and Ben, and knew in my heart that it wasn't right. I didn't fit in 1898. I turned my head at the last moment. His lips met my wet cheek.

'I don't belong here.'

'You belong with me,' he said, 'if you want to.'

'I wish I could stay,' I said. 'I want to more than anything, but there's Armuth.'

I paused. 'Did Dad really say in the papers she could be my guardian?'

Julien smiled. 'She is nice?'

I frowned, then nodded. 'I think she's been trying to tell me something about all this, but she kept stopping.'

Julien took my hand in his. 'Perhaps she thought you were happy with this Aunt Cece and did not want to interfere.'

My mouth dropped open. *That* was Aunt Cece's game! That's why she'd been so nice!

'But I'm not happy,' I said. 'They hate me and I don't want to live with them. I'd much rather live with Armuth.' I stopped. 'What? Why are you smiling?'

Julien took both my hands in his. 'I am smiling,' Julien said, 'because you have a home to go to and it is my home and we will share it even though we will not be together.'

I frowned. 'What do you mean?'

He smiled. 'I said that the deeds of the sale have been drawn up, but they are not yet signed.' He looked at the door hidden in the wall, then back at me. 'I understand,' he said gently, 'about you not feeling as if you belong here with me.'

Hearing it like that stung like salt on a cut.

'I don't want to go,' I said. 'Not really.' I looked back at my door, the mirror hiding behind it.

'I know,' he said. He clasped the papers. 'Whatever that woman's reasons for keeping it from you, this is your home as much as it is mine.' He grinned. 'Claim it!'

Chapter Forty-Four

I stared at the papers and shook my head.

'It won't be easy,' I said.

He took my hand in his and squeezed it. 'Nothing worth having is easy.'

I turned away and looked out the window. My heart hurt like it was full of gravel. I'd felt so light after telling him the truth, but I wanted the dream too – I wanted that future, the one where he kissed me, not the one where I had to confront Aunt Cece and Armuth and fight for what was mine.

'I was lost without you,' Julien said behind me, 'and alone and dying. You changed everything. You are extraordinary.'

I snorted. 'No one else thinks that,' I said, picking up the papers. 'And it's only going to get worse now I know about these.'

Julien nodded with a wry smile. 'And I suspect my life with my uncle will not always be so simple as it is at this moment. Especially now I am the heir.'

'But what if Armuth hates me? What if she says no?' I picked at my nails. 'I upset her. I said things . . .'

'You won't know if you do not ask.'

I looked up. 'It would be easier if I stayed here,' I said, not looking at him.

'But not right,' he answered gently. 'You told me that.'

It was true; I had said it. Staying here was just a dream; an amazing one with embroidered dresses and the promise of more kisses, but a dream all the same.

'Help me to the window,' he said.

He was still a little weak and kept one arm round my shoulders to hold himself up. It made my skin tingle. We peered out into the early morning and his face broke into a wide smile as he surveyed the lands he was going to inherit. He pointed out where the new walnut grove would be and my jaw dropped. I'd expected to see the spindly old trees and yellowing lawn, but the land was green and lush and stretched as far as the horizon. The tall grasses swayed in the breeze, making the trees look as if they sprouted from a green sea. I closed my eyes and let the sunlight fall on my face, allowing myself one more run through the tall grass, feeling the dew on my fingertips, my long embroidered skirt heavy and trying to trip me up.

'It is Philippe's idea to make oil from the walnuts. He was an expert, one of only a handful in his field of study, though he said his method was unique. And he taught me. Now I can make it happen, thanks to you.' He squeezed my shoulder. 'It is a good legacy. I will honour it. Will you claim yours?'

I opened my eyes and Julien's mouth was there. I felt his breath on my lips and a shiver ran down my spine. I heard his heart beating or it could have been mine, I don't know. He leant closer. I leant closer. I let my lips brush his, feather light. Then I moved back. His eyes stayed shut. 'Again,' I wanted to say, but I didn't. I knew if I did, I wouldn't leave. Not ever.

'I don't know how you came here, but I am glad that you did,' he said and opened his eyes. 'This house will be your home, and that makes me happy.' He took my hands in his. 'I faced my troubles and survived them, because of *you.*'

I held still.

'Because of you.'

He waited. I think he was making sure I'd heard him properly.

'Now you must do the same.'

His words were gentle, his eyes kind. He was the boy in my dream, or he would be, and I still wanted that so much I felt it pull at me like an ache, but he was right,

– 251 –

however much I wished he wasn't.

He leant in and kissed me again, his lips crushing mine this time. Then he let go and made his way back to his bed.

'But I'll be alone,' I said.

He sat on the edge of his bed, a little out of breath, and smiled.

'But you can survive it,' he said. 'You saved me, Angela; now it is time to save yourself.' He swung his legs round. 'Being alone, you have taught me that it is not the worst thing. You are strong and brave. You stood up to my uncle! To the whole village! You are a survivor, do you not see? You can do anything.'

I heard a scuffling noise from beyond the other doorway. Someone was coming.

'It is the doctor,' Julien said, looking at me.

It was time to go. We both knew it, but I couldn't move.

We listened to laboured footsteps, several of them, getting closer and closer.

'But it's not my home,' I said quietly, 'not really.'

He smiled. 'Home is wherever *you* are,' he said.

I rushed to him and we hugged so forcefully he almost fell over. We both laughed and a smile found its way to my lips.

We heard voices outside. He pressed the papers into my hands. 'Go!' he whispered and I ran to my door and opened it. The mirror was pushed aside and vibrating. I peeked through and saw the attic room was empty. No Aunt Cece. The mirror began to ripple furiously, as if it was alive, as if it was waiting for me. I stepped through quickly and turned back for one last look. There was a knock at Julien's other door and the handle rattled. Julien raised his eyebrows.

'Happy birthday,' I said, then shut the door that separated us before I could change my mind. The mirror slid across so fast it nearly took my hand off. It thunked into place then gave a half sigh, half groan as it settled. I didn't need to try pushing it to know it wouldn't open again, no matter how hard I tried.

I stared at my reflection, except this time I could also see right through to Julien. He was smiling. I felt as if I could touch the rays of sunlight filtering across his room. I saw his head turn, watched the door to the tower begin to open, then the mirror bulged towards me. I stepped back, blinked, and then all I could see was my own reflection. I was in the old attic room and he was gone.

I covered the mirror with a dustsheet. It blended back into the room as if it had never been found, as if it didn't even exist. I opened the door to the hallway. Julien said I had a home to go to. I took a deep breath and clutched the papers. It was time to confront Aunt Cece and Armuth, and find out if that was true.

Chapter Forty-Five

I opened the door, stepped into the hallway – and gasped. The floors were polished to a shine, nearly blinding me. Early morning light beamed through open shutters all along the corridor. Chatter bubbled up from downstairs.

It was like I was in a different house.

I tiptoed to the top of the stairs and leant over the rail. A huge chandelier dangled above me, its delicate glass twinkling and refracting jewel-like patterns. I didn't remember it being there before.

I hovered, shifting from foot to foot and biting my bottom lip. Then I took a deep breath and slowly headed down. I trailed my hand along the shiny bannister that smelt of pine and stared open-mouthed at the portraits on the walls that looked brand new, even though the people's hairstyles and fancy clothes were clearly from over a hundred years ago. The chandelier light twinkled over their gold-black frames and the oils looked so fresh I could pick out the brush strokes. My stomach began to flip over.

I searched for Julien in the pictures, for his mother and his Uncle Nicolas, but I couldn't find them. There was a man in a uniform, a blue top with a red stripe down one side and bright red trousers, then another of a pretty young blond girl with a thousand ringlets in a pale pink dress with a hundred frills. There were group family portraits, everyone stiff backed and glaring at the artist, and I counted three pictures of horses standing in fields and two of what looked like the same brown and white whiskery dog, his tail standing to attention.

I followed them one by one down the stairs, straining on tiptoe to check the highest ones, then I froze.

Someone was humming.

I looked behind me, then back in front. I shuffled closer to the edge of the first floor landing and peered round.

The voice broke into song and it was coming from Armuth and Herman's son's room.

I inched a little closer and the stair beneath me creaked. I leapt back just as Armuth walked out.

She was wearing the same woolly brown dress she wore when I first met her, the same belt cinched round her middle and the same squeaky orthopaedic shoes, but her face was different. She was actually smiling. She took two steps forward then one back and did a sort of twirl. I leant against the bannister, rubbed my hands over my face and looked again, but she was still smiling.

With a half song, half shout, she called over the balcony to someone below, something about *petit déjeuner*. My mouth watered. Breakfast. I swallowed. I was right behind her. If she turned round now, she'd see me. I kept as still as possible and tried not to think about hot croissants.

'*Alors, Angela?*'

She'd seen me. My stomach flipped. The time had come.

'Quickly,' she said, picking up a stack of folded bedding from a chair, 'or your cousins will have eaten every *pain au chocolat*.'

She nodded for me to go ahead of her, but I didn't move.

'Angela?'

I lifted my chin and held out the papers. She glanced at them. A brief red flushed her cheeks before disappearing, then she nodded enthusiastically.

'Good news. You found them.'

'Huh?'

I frowned. First of all she should've been freaking out that I was upstairs and second of all, I'd just showed her the papers that she and Aunt Cece had been hiding from me.

Armuth transferred the bed sheets to one arm, took the papers and placed them on top. She put her other arm round my shoulders and walked us both down the stairs.

'I have been looking for my copy everywhere.' She smiled. 'I wanted to tell you so much.' She squeezed my shoulder and we stopped. 'Do you understand them? Do you need me to translate?'

I shook my head.

'I wanted to say something to you, to tell you, but your aunt said not to talk to you. She said you had been through so much and you were unwell, troubled . . .'

My jaw dropped. Aunt Cece had said *I* wasn't to talk to *Armuth*!

'It's okay,' I said, blowing out a breath. 'I mean, I understand them now.'

'I didn't want to sell,' Armuth said, 'but I thought perhaps it would be best, for you and for me.'

I shook my head. 'That's not Aunt Cece's plan,' I said. 'She wants to sell it. She wants the money all for herself.'

I ran my hand over the bannister. It felt cool beneath my touch, smooth and polished. 'I love this house,' I said in a quiet voice. 'I don't want to leave.'

Armuth looked up at the chandelier then back at me.

'I do not want to leave either.' She tightened her arm around my shoulders so that she was practically hugging me. 'I knew it!'

I felt dizzy.

'When you said Herman had given you the sewing box, I knew. He was telling me something. He was telling me to trust you.' Her voice lowered. 'I did not know I had a brother until last year, but we wrote letters.' She smiled gently. 'Your father was very kind. The business fell apart after Herman died. I could not manage the grove by myself and I could not afford to hire anyone. I did not know what to do. Your father wrote to say he might have some ideas, that perhaps he could help, but we never got the chance to meet.' Her mouth tightened. 'And then Cece told me again and again that it was time to let go. She said the house was too much for one person and I should think of your future. But all the time she was thinking of herself.' She shook herself. 'It does not matter now.' She took a breath and smiled again. 'I am happy that if I did not get to meet your father, I have a niece, yes?'

I looked up at her.

'You will tell me about him, yes?'

She seemed to want an answer, but I couldn't find any words at all so I nodded.

She let go of me and gathered the sheets in both arms. 'Please know that this is your home. In fact,' she turned at the bottom of the stairs, 'I would like you to visit every holiday, unless . . .'

Just then Kitty and Fliss bolted past into the kitchen, letting the door slam behind them. Armuth turned to follow.

Unless what, I wanted to shout. Unless what?

'We will make a plan together, yes?' Armuth said, wedging the kitchen door open with one hip. 'There is still time for us to talk.' She turned and winked. 'All the time in the world, yes?'

I shrugged, then nodded, but I had no idea what she meant. I looked at the clock in the hall. It was way past breakfast time so I knew we were supposed to be leaving any minute. I stared after Armuth.

I'd saved Julien and stopped the fire; now the house had changed and Armuth too. But something was niggling me. I shook my head trying to make the pieces fall into place. Then I smacked a palm to my forehead. The antibiotics!

I remembered the paper bag left neatly on Julien's bedside table. In the rush to leave I'd left it behind. I turned and ran straight back up the stairs. The door to Armuth's son's room was ajar. It still looked empty and unused, but the shutters and windows were wide open, the wooden floor polished and the room smelt of sheets that had been left to dry in the sun.

I pulled out the bottom drawer of the cabinet. The medicines were gone. I bit my lip. Of course they were, I'd taken them. I shut the drawer and sat on the bed, the springs squawking like a bird. I could hear Armuth singing downstairs. My hands felt empty without the papers but as I stared at the cabinet, I knew that was the past. I was ready to find Armuth and ask her to explain what she meant about me staying. I stood up and the bed squawked again, but standing in the middle of the doorway was the last person I wanted to see. She stood with her arms crossed, one eyebrow raised. It was Aunt Cece.

Chapter Forty-Six

'Breakfast,' she said, almost without moving her lips. Then she raised one corner of her mouth in a half smile that reminded me of Kaa from *The Jungle Book*. 'Then you can say goodbye to this house,' she said, darting her eyes from the cupboard to the bed and the chair as if she was pricing them up before turning on her heels and walking away. I followed her to the door, then with a frown at the cabinet I ran down the stairs after her.

'I'm not going.'

Aunt Cece's back stiffened. She stopped, then without turning round her heels began clip-clopping down the stairs.

'I said I'm not going!'

Aunt Cece reached a hand to pat her stiff hair, which looked like a hairsprayed helmet, and totally ignored me.

I followed her. 'I know what you did. What you *tried*

to do.' My heart was beating quadruple time, like a herd of wild horses in my chest. 'I've read the papers.'

Aunt Cece reached the bottom of the stairs and stopped with her back to me.

'It's not what Mum and Dad wanted.'

She turned to me.

'It's my choice,' I said. 'It's . . .'

I stopped.

Aunt Cece was smiling. Her top lip curled upwards so I could see all her teeth. I stepped back. She patted her hair again and straightened the sleeves of her pale jacket.

'Whatever you think, or say, I'm the only one who wants you, Angela.'

Her voice was so quiet I had to lean in to hear.

'Armuth doesn't want you. Why would she?'

I felt a shiver run up my back as I looked towards the kitchen.

'All you do is upset people.'

Aunt Cece smoothed down her pencil skirt and brushed an invisible speck of dust off it.

I swallowed, remembered what Julien had said. This house was half mine. I had to claim it!

'That's not true,' I said.

Aunt Cece raised one perfectly drawn eyebrow.

'We talked. Armuth knows. She knows I love this house and I'll fight for it. I'll fight you if I have to. It's what Mum and Dad wanted for me. You can't stop me. You can't stop us.'

Aunt Cece's head fell back and an awful high-pitched hitching noise came out of her mouth. Her shoulders jogged up and down. She looked at me and I realised she was laughing.

'How can you possibly love this house?' she said. 'You've only been here a few days.'

I thought of Julien and Herman and everything I'd learnt.

'I know all about the house,' I said.

I looked at the paintings on the wall and the hundreds of tiny diamonds of light from the chandelier spinning across the stairs between us.

'I know its history. I know more than you ever will.'

Aunt Cece laughed even harder and pretended to wipe her eyes. 'More stories.'

'I won't let you sell it,' I said. 'And neither will Armuth.'

Aunt Cece stopped laughing.

I gulped.

'This house is half mine,' I said, but my voice quivered, 'and I choose . . .'

Aunt Cece interrupted me. Her voice low and syrupy, her eyes flashing and her lip curled, not into a fake smile this time, but something that made her nostrils flare.

'You are a child. What you will choose is me or another children's home.'

I pressed my bitten nails into my palms. 'That's not true. That's not what the papers say.'

Aunt Cece dug into her handbag and brought out some papers. Armuth's copy!

I gasped. She was the one who'd taken them from the dresser. I thought back to her chasing me. She'd had something in her dressing gown pocket then.

'It's what I say,' she said, brandishing them at me, 'and it's what Armuth will say when I've finished with her, believe me.'

Aunt Cece snapped her mouth shut then turned to the kitchen, but someone had been watching, someone had been listening and someone had something to say.

Chapter Forty-Seven

Armuth stood in the doorway to the kitchen, Aunt Cece's papers in her hand.

'What *I* will say is that Angela is most welcome here.'

'Armuth,' Aunt Cece said with a little laugh. 'I'm so glad you found my papers. And we've just enough time for you to sign both copies before we go.' She reached into her handbag for a pen, clicked it and held it out.

I frowned. It was as if the last ten minutes hadn't happened. I looked from Aunt Cece to Armuth and waited. My stomach rolled.

'Breakfast,' Armuth said.

She glanced at the pen in Aunt Cece's outstretched hand, then turned and walked into the kitchen.

I peeked out of the corner of my eye at my aunt who looked at her pen as if it had upset her, put it in her handbag with the papers, snapped the clasp shut and clip-clopped after Armuth, muttering about breakfast first then signing. Two seconds later I followed them.

In the kitchen everyone was busy piling into the massive plate of croissants and *pains au chocolat*. I looked around for Herman, but he wasn't there. I was itching to see him and ask him what he knew about Julien and his uncle. In fact, I had about a hundred questions for him. I wanted to check the books in the library too, and look for the new ones Julien had mentioned he was planning. I wanted to finish my talk with Armuth as well, but most of all, I wanted to hear what she had to say to Cece.

'I found your copy, Cece,' Armuth said, smiling at me and helping herself to jam. 'Strange how mine disappeared . . .' she paused, 'and then reappeared.'

There was an empty seat next to Armuth and I sat down.

'But no matter.' She nodded to the plate of pastries and I took a croissant. 'I will not sell.'

Aunt Cece stared at Armuth as I broke my croissant in two.

'I will *never* sell.'

Something warm bloomed in my chest. I grinned. Aunt Cece looked from Armuth to me, her eyes narrowing to tiny pinpricks.

'We are making a plan,' Armuth said, and gave me a one-armed hug. Her other was busy with the butter knife.

'But you can't possibly manage all on your own,' Aunt Cece said, her eyebrows up to the ceiling now. I don't think I was the only one that heard the sour note on her tongue. She had her pen out again and was clicking it on-off, on-off.

I looked at Armuth.

'The house is in excellent shape,' Armuth said, then she smiled at me. 'And perhaps I won't be alone.'

Aunt Cece looked like she'd swallowed a lemon. I stuffed a bit of pastry into my mouth.

'Well,' she said, looking at Uncle Vaughn for help. He shrugged his shoulders, held his hands up.

'Well, we'll see about this,' she said, scraping her chair as she got up. She threw the pen into her bag. 'Come on, girls.'

'But Armuth only just started telling us the story,' Kitty said.

'Yes, finish the story of the house, Armuth,' Fliss said, with a quick look at her mum. 'Please?'

'We're leaving,' Aunt Cece said, her hands gripping the back of her chair as she turned to me. 'And you're coming with us, Angela.'

I looked at Armuth who was just about to say something when Kitty spoke. 'Please, Mum.'

She and Fliss turned to their dad. 'Please, please, please, please, please?'

He grinned and put his hands up. 'What's five minutes?'

Aunt Cece nodded curtly.

'Well,' Armuth said, giving my hand a pat, 'as I was saying, this house is here all because of his story. History, I suppose you could say.'

She chuckled and Kitty, Fliss and I smiled with her. It was infectious. Uncle Vaughn reached for another pastry. Aunt Cece, still standing, picked up her coffee cup and sipped it like it was poisonous. I grabbed another two croissants and broke them in half, hoovering up the flakes with my fingers.

'It was the boy's story, right?' Kitty said.

Fliss screwed her eyes. 'And he's your great-great-great-great-grandfather,' she said.

I stopped chewing.

'Back when the house was doomed,' Kitty said, laughing, with jazz hands.

I choked on my pastry.

'Stop interrupting and let her finish,' Aunt Cece said, banging her empty cup on the table. 'Then we can get out of here.'

Uncle Vaughn was still laughing at Kitty.

Armuth beamed. She was shaking her head. 'No,' she said to Fliss, 'my great-great-however-many-times-great-grandfather was the boy's uncle.' She turned to Kitty. 'And yes,' she said, 'the house was indeed doomed.'

Then she looked at me. 'The books tell us that the boy saved the house, but we Brodeurs don't need them because we know the story by heart,' she said, her chin up. 'Each generation passes it on to the next, along with the surname. It is most wonderful.'

She paused, making sure we were all listening, but she didn't need to. You could hear a pin drop. I pushed my plate away.

'Because of the boy and his story, the house is going to live again.'

My heart was hammering. I pulled my chair closer.

Armuth clapped her hands. 'I cannot keep it in. I am delighted to tell you that I have been offered the opportunity to sell the walnut oil from the grove at a very prestigious market in Paris!'

'Walnut oil?' I said, frowning. The trees outside were all dead the last time I looked. Then I thought about what Julien said about his stepfather's plans and broke into a huge smile.

'Oh,' I said. 'He did it. He really did it. He made the walnut grove.'

'Duh,' Kitty said, 'she told us that story last night.'

When I looked at Kitty, Fliss joined in.

'The one about the boy and the angel?'

I could feel my face reddening.

Kitty tossed her ponytail. 'The boy recovered amazingly

from some, like, hideous disease,' she said, pulling a face. 'And he met an angel or whatever and he planted the walnut grove in her honour.'

My skin tingled. My lips felt like they were humming.

'What boy?' I said. I had to hear them say his name, but no one answered. They were too busy talking over each other.

'What about the boy?' I shouted.

Everyone went quiet. Kitty rolled her eyes and pretended to stick her fingers down her throat with sound effects. Fliss giggled until Aunt Cece gave them both one of her looks. Fliss mouthed a silent sorry to me.

Armuth explained with a twinkle in her eye. 'He believed he owed his very life to a ghost girl.'

I shivered.

'The books call her, *mon ange*, my angel.'

She turned to me, smiled then whispered. 'My *ange*, my angel, my Angela?'

I gulped.

She winked.

'What?' I said, looking to see if anyone else had heard or seen, but Kitty and Fliss were arguing over the last croissant, and Aunt Cece and Uncle Vaughn had got up from the table.

I turned back to Armuth, but she was tidying up the kitchen and facing the other way.

'Right, finish packing, Angela, and meet us in the car in ten minutes,' Aunt Cece said, both hands on the back of my chair.

'No,' I said. 'I'm not going. I need to speak to Armuth.'

'You can't stay with her right now, Angela. There's paperwork. Things have to be organised.' She leant over and lowered her voice. 'And plenty of time for people to change their minds.'

I shook my head. The floor felt as if it was shifting. 'But . . .'

Aunt Cece had moved off to corner Armuth. So I did the next best thing. I ran away.

Chapter Forty-Eight

I ran out of the kitchen, across the hall and straight through the open front door. Outside the gravel crunched under my feet like it was freshly laid, no bare patches now. I ran across, then stopped at the barn, which had been transformed into a working outbuilding three times its original size. Peeping inside a door wedged open I found giant wheels turning, a large funnel revolving in the centre and a row of cast iron kettles. It was loud, the machinery clashing, grinding and whirring. The whole place smelt nutty and inside on stacked shelves I found trays of walnuts in various stages of colour, from a rich brown to a burnt black. It smelt like Christmas. I crept close to touch one and it left black smudges on my fingertips like charcoal. I smiled. Then the funnel screamed and I ran back outside.

I raced through the tall swishing grass behind the

barn, following the trail of wildflowers till the grove lay in front of me. It spread as far as I could see and looked just like my dream. I grinned from ear to ear and laughed out loud.

The trees were lush, their branches spreading out like welcoming arms. Some laid their branches down into the grass so they seemed to disappear, until you couldn't tell what was tree and what was grass.

I ran between trees blending into one another, each branch laying across to the next, and the next, like they were holding hands. Their leaves were bright green and the walnuts hung in heavy clusters. Small birds twittered and swooped above the canopy and something scurried about in the grass on my left. If I shut my eyes I could almost feel heavy skirts around my legs, hear Julien counting.

'Angelaaaaaaa?'

I shook myself.

Kitty was shouting for me. I turned and peered through the trees to the house and noticed there weren't any boards across any of the windows now. I blew out a breath. No boards and one, two, three, four, five, six, seven, eight, nine windows! And the tower, it was there, wrapped round the side of the house with russet red leaves winding themselves up to the balcony – the balcony where I'd stood and shouted to the villagers.

'Angela!' Aunt Cece screeched.

I turned away from the house.

The deeper I ran into the orchard, the wetter the long grass got till I came to the graveyard. There were only a handful of graves there now and all were well tended. They stood tall, gently weathered by time, but with the grass trimmed neatly around them in a circle. I quickly searched for the right one and found it towards the back outer edge. It stood proudly upright with two graves slightly behind it for Julien's mother and stepfather, and another two on its left for his Uncle Nicolas and Nicolas's wife. I ran my fingertips over the dates inscribed and smiled because his grave showed me Julien lived a long life.

A car horn beeped, but I ignored it.

Julien had said I was a survivor. Well, I'd survived the fire, but I didn't think that was what he meant. Not really. I think he meant I could survive surviving, even if I was the only one left. I hadn't realised that till now.

I closed my eyes and let the memories of my mum, dad and baby brother come. It was difficult at first. The first images were the ones I dreaded, the ones that punched a hole where my heart should be. I saw my dad under the smoking duvet, a shapeless monster with bloodshot eyes. My head filled with a smoke-filled room for my mum and Ben, with the walls engulfed in red, orange and yellow flames. My heart began to beat faster and faster as the panic that fed my nightmare rose up in my throat. I held on to the grave with both hands, forced myself to take long, slow, deep breaths. I remembered what Julien had said. I could survive this.

As I let the smoke clear, to my surprise, I saw my family how they'd looked in the studio portrait we'd had done a few months before the fire.

'This is totally corny, Dad,' I'd said at the time, but I was glad of the memory now. I didn't have a copy of the photo. I didn't have anything from my old home except for some bits I kept in the bottom of my rucksack – a T-shirt and the pyjamas I'd been wearing that night that were so singed I couldn't wear them any more. Out of all the photos, all the albums sitting in a box in the attic, all the paintings stuck on the fridge, all the school pictures my mum insisted were hung along the wall near the front door, this was the one I remembered now. I saw my mum's long, curly hair and tired, but happy smile. I could see my dad's cheesy grin as he mugged up to the camera, one arm round me as I leant back into him, looking embarrassed, and Ben, a curled shrimp in my mother's arms, a shock of hair sticking up like he was the world's youngest punk.

A smile made its way to my lips and quiet tears salted my face.

'Goodbye,' I whispered to them. My hand brushed the top of Julien's gravestone. 'I love you.'

More tears came, but I didn't wipe them. It felt like they were washing the bad stuff away. In my head I traced the outline of my family on the photo. My mum wearing her blue jersey and the chunky silver necklace she wore for best, my dad's maroon jumper that was worn through at the elbows. He'd insisted on wearing it, telling Mum the holes wouldn't show in the picture, and they didn't, but I liked knowing they were there. Ben was wearing the fluffy bear suit someone from Mum's school had bought him. She'd said she'd show the picture to his girlfriend when he was fifteen to embarrass him. I squeezed my eyes tight. She'd never get the chance.

'I'll do my best, okay?' I whispered to them. 'Even though it's just me now.'

My breath hitched. I swallowed, wiped away a last tear, then opened my eyes.

Sunshine poured through the trees, lighting up a little dell around me. The sky was a deep, endless blue and I could feel the old solid stone of the grave beneath my hands.

Julien had said that home was wherever I was.

Armuth had said we would make a plan.

I didn't want to go to another kids' home and I didn't want to leave the house. I'd told Cece I'd fight her for it, but I thought about what she'd said, about all the paperwork and time for people to change their minds. She was probably right about the paperwork, but maybe it wasn't too late to talk to Armuth.

A car horn beeped loud and angry. Running away wasn't going to solve anything anyway. I had to start making that plan – right now.

Chapter Forty-Nine

I ran back into the house. On the wall an ornate clock ticked the seconds away. I stood at the bottom of the stairs and yelled for Armuth. Nothing. I ran into the kitchen. The table had been cleared and scrubbed. I checked the annexe, but she wasn't there either. Outside the car horn beeped.

I checked the small salon, then the library. The door creaked open and I gasped. The whole room was filled from floor to ceiling with books. The glass cases stood polished and shining. The shutters were open, letting sunlight flood into the room, lighting up a chessboard sitting in the centre of the table. Julien's chessboard!

I ran over. The chessboard looked old, but beautifully preserved, as if someone had looked after it, cherished it. One pawn was out on each side, mirroring the other, as if a new game had just begun.

'Angela?' A sweet, strong voice called my name.

With a grin I left the chessboard and ran back into the hall, down the corridor, careering into my room – but she wasn't there. I saw my rucksack, but instead of sitting on the floor where I'd left it, it was on the bed, all packed and ready to go. Next to it was the sewing box.

I popped my head out the door, but Herman was nowhere to be seen either so I sat down next to the box and stroked its smooth wooden top, smiling. I longed to open it and start sewing, but the horn beeped three times, one after the other. I sighed.

I stuffed the box into my rucksack, then just as I swung it onto one shoulder, a little key fell out of the wardrobe door. I picked it up. It was the same ceramic key as before, but where the picture on the fob had been scratched before, it was crystal clear now.

It was a drawing of me.

It had my messy hair exactly right and the blouse I'd sewn myself. Something about the way I was looking away, at the window drawn behind, made me gasp. This was how Julien saw me. I clasped the key to my heart. He must have drawn it and had it made. I shut my eyes and smiled, wondering what else I'd find in the house now, what other things would make me feel like I felt right this minute, like I was warm inside and out and . . . home. I laughed, opened my eyes and my hand, and gazed at the drawing of me. It felt like Julien was here.

I put the little key back in the wardrobe, then raced out into the corridor. I still had to find Armuth.

The floors were polished to such a shine that I kept slipping and everything smelt of air freshener. I checked the kitchen again, but she wasn't there.

'Armuth?'

I ran past the salon then the library and even checked a funny little panelled door in the hallway I hadn't noticed till now, but she wasn't anywhere.

The car horn beeped loud and long.

I dragged my feet towards the front door and stopped at the foot of the staircase and stared at a round, bobbled bit of wood at the top of the post. It wasn't smooth any more – it was a walnut! I smiled. Of course.

I glanced up at the stairs behind it. Maybe Armuth was up there? I dropped my bag and had taken just one step when there was a polite cough behind me. I turned and there she was.

'There you are, Angela,' she said.

Her eyes sparkled. Her voice was soft and warm. She rocked on her squeaky shoes.

'Thank you,' she added.

I had so many questions to ask her, but what came out instead was, 'For the papers?'

She shook her head and took my hands in hers. 'I am

glad you found them and I am glad I got the chance to do the right thing.' She looked around her. 'This is more than just a house.' She smiled. 'And I would like you to be here with me.' She glanced up the stairs. 'This is your home now, your legacy as much as mine and we will look after it together, yes?'

I felt something swell inside me.

'I will write to you and your . . .' She frowned. 'Mrs Morrison?'

I swallowed and nodded.

'I will draw up new papers. I will send a copy and we will make a plan.' She paused. 'I will apply to be your legal guardian.' She looked away for a moment. 'If that is what you want. It is your choice, of course, but I would very much like it if you –'

'Yes!' I said, interrupting. 'Yes!'

She smiled, and laughter bubbled out of me.

'Yes! I mean, I'd like that, so much, please.'

I paused. It felt a little presumptuous to say I wanted to live here with her forever, but I totally wanted to live here with her forever.

Armuth smiled, nodded and gave me a hug, cushioning me against her. I didn't even notice the scratchy dress. I felt like I was home. A new home, but a home all the same.

'Good,' she said as she straightened up. 'Then we have

a plan, yes? You will come to live here. With me.'

I nodded like my head was on a spring. She let me go and I picked up my rucksack and slung it over my shoulder.

That's when I saw something move. Out of the corner of my eye one of the large tapestries ruffled in the breeze, except I couldn't feel a breeze. I looked closer and the whole tapestry rippled. I could hear whispering. The embroidered lady in a hooped skirt and the man in a top hat standing next to a carriage quivered, and in the dark space behind, one of the wall panels began to slide open.

Chapter Fifty

'Angela!'

Aunt Cece's screech made me jump, and when I looked back at the tapestry it lay flat against the wall, full of threads and nothing else. The couple were still.

'Ah, Angela,' Armuth said, clasping her hands behind her. She followed my gaze, her eyes twinkling. 'What adventures will be here for you when you come back, yes?'

'Angela!' Aunt Cece yelled for the second time.

I took a step towards the tapestry, then back towards the front door. I wanted to see what was behind the hanging more than anything and I wanted to ask Armuth what other secrets the house was keeping. Did she know about the mirror?

'You know, he never married,' she said quietly.

I looked up at her.

'The boy who saved the house.' She paused. 'Perhaps you saw his grave in the orchard?'

I swallowed.

'He lived a long life,' I said.

'Yes,' she said, nodding and smiling gently. 'The history books say he dedicated his life to the estate, but we the family always suspected that no one quite measured up to his *ange*, yes?'

My mouth dropped, but before I could say a word, she was ushering me outside. Uncle Vaughn was waiting. He took my rucksack and wedged it into the car boot. I looked back at Armuth but she was waving goodbye.

'You promise?' I said.

She smiled. 'I promise, *mon ange*. I will write to them today.'

I ran back to her and we hugged.

She clasped my hands. 'We are family.'

'Come on, Angela!' Aunt Cece said.

Uncle Vaughn had got in the driver's seat and shut his door.

'Angela!'

I jogged to the car, pulled open the nearest door and jumped in straight onto Kitty.

'Owwwww!'

'Sorry.'

She lifted up a foot and I grimaced. I'd broken the

buckle off her new boots. I held still, waiting for the hysterics, but instead she turned away from me, shut her door and stared out the window.

'Doesn't matter,' she muttered. 'Dad'll buy me another pair on one of his stupid credit cards.'

Her shoulders began to jerk and I realised she was crying.

'I'm sorry, Kitty,' I said and was about to say something more when Fliss pulled on my cardigan. She shook her head, then nodded to her mum and dad arguing in the front.

Armuth was still waving as Uncle Vaughn turned the car round, and I suddenly remembered I hadn't said goodbye to Herman. In fact, I hadn't seen him at all since I left Julien. I had so many questions for him. Was it all a plan to help Armuth and the house? Would I still see him now? I hoped so.

I twisted round to look out of the back window and saw him standing tall behind Armuth. He gave me a grave nod, then seemed to fade into the morning sunlight until I could only see Armuth waving. Then, as the car rumbled down the drive, I couldn't see either of them any more.

The car passed through the gate and into the village. I turned around and hugged my knees at the thought of coming back.

Aunt Cece switched on the radio and French pop filled the car. I stared at the plane trees lining the road, then I closed my eyes and let the tree shapes flit yellow and red across my eyelids. Kitty and Fliss had put their earphones in, their music soft, almost soothing, but when I heard my name I froze.

'She must have got to Armuth, told her some story to make her change her mind. Now she's ruined everything,' Aunt Cece huffed. 'I should own that house. Me, not a twelve year old.'

Uncle Vaughn shushed her, but it was too late; I'd heard everything. My eyes flicked open. I felt the familiar stir of anger rolling in the pit of my stomach, but I didn't push it down this time.

'Why did you do it?'

Aunt Cece stiffened at my words.

'Why did you hide those papers from me?'

'What?'

'You hid the papers. The ones with my dad's name on. And you tried to get Armuth to sell the house so it would be all yours.'

Fliss took out her earphones and shook her head at me.

'I don't know what you're talking about, Angela,' Aunt Cece said, waving a hand in my direction.

'But you do,' I said. 'You knew what it said about my

– 286 –

dad and about him wanting me to choose who could be my guardian, and you hid them from me.'

She bristled as if she was sitting on pins.

'Why did you try to choose for me? You hate me!'

Uncle Vaughn coughed. 'Oh, now, Angela, we don't hate you.'

He tried to pat his wife, but she shifted away from him.

'And you were never planning on letting me live with you, were you? You just said that so I wouldn't get in your way while you tried to steal the house.'

Kitty and Fliss gasped, both listening now. Aunt Cece coughed like she was choking on something.

'Now, now, I think we should all relax,' Uncle Vaughn said. 'Stealing's a bit of a strong word.'

'And I think we'd all like to know what you were doing in my things,' Aunt Cece said, her voice dripping with a sickly sweetness. 'Isn't that stealing?'

Fliss clutched my arm. I put my hand on hers and squeezed. I wasn't going to get her into trouble.

'Nobody hates anyone, Angela,' Uncle Vaughn said. 'And I don't think this matters now, does it, eh?' he added. 'It's all worked out for the best.'

He half smiled, half grimaced through the rear-view mirror. Aunt Cece huffed and moved so far away from him she was practically welded to her door.

I wasn't so sure. Right at that moment I think Aunt Cece hated me and him.

Uncle Vaughn slowed the car. His eyes met mine in the mirror.

'You and Armuth, eh?' he said. He glanced at his wife then turned back to the wheel. 'You'll make a good team. Keep each other company.'

Aunt Cece's back was as stiff as a broom.

'Perhaps you'll invite me to stay some time? I'll be needing somewhere pretty soon.'

He snorted then shook his head, as if he'd made a joke.

I sat back. Kitty was staring at me with one of her earphones out, the other providing tinny background music. Fliss squeezed my arm. Kitty saw it and stared at her sister, but Fliss didn't let go. I wondered if we'd be friends now. Uncle Vaughn revved the car and we hit the cobbled lanes of the first village.

I closed my eyes and remembered Julien's words: *You're a survivor, Angela. You can do anything.*

He was right. I was a survivor.

I smiled.

I wasn't on my own any more, either. I thought of what Armuth had said as she clasped my hands.

We are family.

I felt something warm spread through my chest.

Home. I had a home.

I understood it now. Home was wherever I was, but it felt good to be sharing it with Armuth and with Julien. Herman too.

I thought about what Armuth had said about adventures waiting for me and grinned. It felt like my adventures were just beginning.

Epilogue

Article taken from, *L'Aurore* newspaper, 1901.

TYPHOID FEVER
– A DOCTOR'S GREAT DISCOVERY.

Dr Chantemesse, of Paris, claims to have discovered a new serum, which will prevent and cure that much-to-be-dreaded malady, typhoid fever.

The world has been awaiting the results of Dr Chantemesse's experiments with this wonderful life-saving serum, which he created in late 1898.

Now, after three years of work in French hospitals, with funds provided by the Council of Paris (and a private benefactor in Tours) the distinguished doctor's paper proves that his treatment is shown to be at 88 per cent effectiveness in curing typhoid fever.

Typhoid has made fearful ravages in France. The statistics collected by the Council of Paris show that out of 12,818,235 inhabitants there have been a total of 55,623 deaths.

Dr Chantemesse firmly believes he has discovered 'a serum that will not only actually cure typhoid fever, but will be a preventive against this dreaded disease as well'.

Cold baths in conjunction with the treatment is said to aid its success.

A Note on Walnuts

Walnuts are part of the tree nut family and have many uses, from dyes made out of the shell to a tea brewed from the leaves that's supposed to cure stomach-aches. Just like in the book, walnuts can also be turned into walnut oil.

Walnut oil makes a lovely salad dressing, but it's also used as a massage oil and you can find it in many skincare products. Even today, most of the production of walnut oil comes from France.

One of the reasons I use the walnut in *Through the Mirror Door* is because, traditionally, walnuts were seen as a symbol of hidden mysteries. Many people believed that eating them could make you more intelligent and help you see things you'd never noticed before . . .

Ancient folklore suggests that if you dream of walnuts it's a sign to follow new opportunities and find your own unique path in life. Though you could always try sleeping under a walnut tree. That's supposed to help you see the future in your dreams!

Acknowledgements

Every book I write is really for me, aged 12, or thereabouts. If I could go back and tell myself one thing it would be this: don't worry, all that reading will change your life one day . . .

. . . and it has!

So a big thanks to my mum, Marie, for teaching me to read very early and instilling in me a lifelong love of books, and to my dad, Bob, for explaining how stories work and why. Thanks to my amazing sister Rachael for telling me I really ought to write some of my stories down and for reading endless drafts of the book. You deserve a dedication (turn the front page, it's there!).

Thank you to my brilliant agent, Bryony Woods, for seeing the potential in *Through the Mirror Door* (and me) so early on. Your enthusiasm is infectious and your editorial advice is always spot on. A huge thank you to everyone at Catnip and Bounce, especially my wonderful editor, Liz Bankes, who gossiped about the characters with me over hot chocolates at the National Theatre and left me little notes of encouragement on my manuscript that kept me smiling. Thank you to my excellent copy editor Melissa Hyder and to Sandrine Gasnier for checking (and correcting!) my French translation. Any mistakes are definitely mine. So very many thanks to Jessica Courtney-Tickle and Will Steele for the gorgeous book cover.

Thanks to the BookBound team of Karen Ball, Sara Grant, Jasmine Richards and Sara O'Connor who so generously shared their knowledge and helped me get the book into shape. They also introduced me to the best group of writers I'm honoured to know. You're all marvellous, thank you for your support. Extra special thanks to Sheila Averbuch and Vivienne Dacosta for generally being amazing and wonderful.

Thanks also to super cheerleaders and friends extraordinaire, Ali Cook and Kate Terence. You said I'd be published and look, you're right! Thanks also to Laura James and Rhian Ivory for their incredible support.

I really must say thank you to my (honestly, very lovely) aunt and uncle for taking me on holiday to a haunted house and sowing the seeds for this story. You're nothing like Aunt Cece and Uncle Vaughn, and neither are my cousins like Kitty and Fliss, thank goodness!

Last, but definitely not least, thank you to Julian Hall for believing my being a writer was, and still is, an excellent idea, and to Freddie . . . You see in between the idea for the book, writing the book and getting it published, I had a baby boy I named Freddie. So thank you, my little one, for sleeping 4–7 a.m. so that I could write and edit *Through the Mirror Door*. The next book is for you, I promise.

Sarah Baker, London, 2016